Murder
and
Madness

3 IN THE MAVIS DAVIS MYSTERY SERIES

SUSAN P. BAKER

2/15/19
To Mosette,
Enjoyed our visit.
Susan P Bak

Refugio Press

MURDER AND MADNESS
No. 3 in the Mavis Davis Mystery Series
Copyright © December 2018 by Susan P. Baker
ISBN: 978-0-9980390-0-8

Interior formatting and design by Laurie Barboza
Cover design by Laurie Barboza

Produced in the United States of America.

For information and/or permission to use excerpts, contact:

Refugio Press
P.O. Box 3937, Galveston, TX 77552.

Books by Susan P. Baker

Novels:

My First Murder, No. 1 in the Mavis Davis mystery series
P.I. Mavis uncovers corruption deep in the heart of Texas while searching for the murderer of a mysterious woman.

The Sweet Scent of Murder, No. 2 in the Mavis Davis mystery series
When her search for a missing teenager turns to murder, Mavis discovers disgusting details about a Houston River Oaks' family.

Murder and Madness, No. 3 in the Mavis Davis mystery series
To fulfill a dying woman's wish, Mavis plunges headfirst into the Galveston island investigation of a grisly ax murder.

Death of a Prince
Mother & daughter criminal defense lawyers defend the alleged murderer of a millionaire plaintiffs' attorney in Galveston, Texas.

Ledbetter Street
With the deck stacked against her, a Galveston mother fights the court system for guardianship of her autistic son.

Suggestion of Death
A father who can't pay his child support investigates the mysterious deaths of deadbeat dads in the Texas Hill Country.

Texas Style Justice
Faced with life altering decisions, an ambitious Texas Hill Country judge must determine what price she is willing to pay to reach her ultimate goal of being appointed to the Supreme Court.

UNAWARE

Galveston, Texas Attorney Dena Armstrong is about to break out from under the two controlling men in her life, unaware that a stranger has other plans for her.

Nonfiction:

Heart of Divorce
Divorce advice especially for those who are considering representing themselves.

Murdered Judges of the 20th Century
True stories of judges killed in America.

https://www.susanpbaker.com

Dedication

For my lovely granddaughter, Abigail, the actress in the family.

CONTENTS

Acknowledgments

The Galveston Novel and Short Story Writers were, as always, wonderful encouragers in the writing of this novel.

Additionally, I want to thank my beta readers: my old friend, Paul Ray Heinrich, Sandy Fields, Judith Shaw, Shari from Canada, Katie Miller Norrell, Leslie Shepherd, Beverlee Smith, and Joeline Webber.

To those of you on my mailing list who sent me comments, I thank you as well.

Of course, I'm always grateful to my multi-talented designer, Laurie Barboza of Design Stash.

Chapter 1

'VE NEVER CARRIED ANYTHING IN MY hands when I've gone to serve papers on someone. I don't want the recipient to guess why I'm there. I keep the court documents folded up in one back pocket, my cell in the other, and my T-shirt or jacket pulled down over them. Ordinarily, a tall, red-haired woman approaching a door won't alarm anyone, so the recipient has the door open and the court papers in hand before he knows it. That's what happened this time.

Except this time, things went south as I was jogging back down the walkway. I wasn't even close to the gate when I heard an odd noise and looked over my shoulder. A monstrous black and gray German Shepherd was racing in my direction. He barked so loudly my hair almost stood on end. He loped toward me, hackles up, and launched himself at my head. Adrenaline swept through my body as I jumped back too late. Huge paws gouged the side of my face. I had no accessible body armor, and although my life didn't pass in front me, I did have visions of being scarred for eternity.

"Get him off me!" I screamed at the man standing on the front porch before I punched the dog in the snout as hard as I could. "Call off your dog, or I'm filing charges." That was an empty threat. Until I got outside the gate, I could do nothing. After kicking the dog and not making much of an impact, I ran as fast as my tennis shoes would carry me in spite of my shaking legs. I'm sure I won the world speed record for reaching the four-foot fence. I high-jumped it instead of exiting through the gate.

In the meantime, I heard, "Beefcake! Down!"

Beefcake? I didn't stop to think too much about the name while focused on escaping. But Beefcake? Really?

"If you come back, Miss Davis, Beefcake will be here to greet you." He let the dog inside the house and slammed the front door at the same time I slammed the door of my Mustang.

Miss Davis? Yes. That's me. Mavis NMI Davis, Private Investigator. Lately, I've been rethinking my career path. I could be a kindergarten teacher. Surely it would be safer. But then again, the stories you hear about kids these days . . .

Something warm rolled down both sides of my throbbing face. Opening the mirror on my visor with shaking hands, I examined my injuries. Perspiration mixed with blood ran down the right side of my face. Luckily, what I'd felt on the left was just plain perspiration. Both eyes were intact, though there was a deep scratch down the right side of my face all the way to my lip and, on closer examination, a nip in the upper part of my ear. My longish hair had protected my neck, thank goodness, but I looked like the wreck of the Hesperus. I licked at my lip and wanted to barf from the metallic taste of my own blood, but I'm not the barfing sort. I dripped all over from perspiration inspired by fear as much as from the summer weather. Oh, how I longed for the first few cold fronts in the fall when the temperature would dip down into the low eighties.

I mopped at the blood with tissues from the tiny package I keep in the glove box. I used to keep my .38 revolver there until my boyfriend, Houston Police Department Lieutenant Ben Sorensen, talked me into keeping it in the safe in my office. What good did that do me? In the future, I'd consider packing my gun when serving court documents.

Though I'd always had a fear of what waited for me in a person's yard when I approached a door, nothing like this had happened since the time I was employed as a social worker and had to remove children from a home. The memory of that incident swept through me, but that's a story for another time.

Yes, I would have felt bad shooting the dog, regardless of whether he was planning on having me for lunch, but in extenuating circumstances, I've found I can do almost anything.

Once the blood was suitably smeared across the side of my face and down my ear, and the throbbing had decreased to a less painful aching, I started the car and pointed it in the direction of my house for a quick change of clothes and to doctor myself. Luckily, I lived near my office. My one-thirty appointment was due to arrive any minute. Lunch would have to wait, I informed my stomach when it snarled at me. It's often impatient, but what can I do when a potential client wants to give me money?

The scratch flared like a burn when the air conditioning hit it. The most I could do was wince and drive faster. The party I'd served lived on the outskirts of Houston, yes, Texas, in a neighborhood some might describe as rough and malodorous. My office was near downtown, quite a dangerous drive away. There are no atheists on the freeways in Houston. The traffic is straight from hell.

Finally arriving and entering my office from the back door, I managed to avoid detection until I'd stashed an additional change of clothes, in case of a future fray, and checked my face in the bathroom mirror to be sure my repair was holding. When I came out, Margaret, my assistant, was waiting for me.

"Oh. My. God." Margaret shrank back. "What happened? Your face. Ugh. Were you in an accident?" Her normally high-pitched voice became almost shrill.

"Don't worry. Nobody's after me, so you don't have to be afraid." I must have looked worse than I thought. After I'd washed my face and bandaged the long scrape, I dabbed some foundation on the lesser scratches. I brushed my hair over my torn ear and applied lipstick. The T-shirt, I had thrown in the trash and replaced with a light pink polo shirt that contrasted nicely with my hair. I thought I didn't look too bad, but I guess she could still tell I'd almost become a well-chewed meal.

Margaret grunted. "Glad someone around here looks normal, namely me."

"For a change." I knew she hadn't been talking about me. Speaking of meals, "What's that I smell coming from the direction of the kitchen? Bacon?" My stomach thundered like an earthquake aftershock.

Still staring at me like she'd seen an apparition, Margaret said, "I'm making a BLT. Want one? Did you not have breakfast again?"

I shook my head. "I meant to."

"And no snacks or lunch?"

"No, Mother. I guess that's why I feel like I'm going to pass out."

"Or from shock and trauma as a result of what happened to you, which you have yet to tell me about." She stood with her hand on her hip.

Sometimes I wasn't sure who was the boss and who was the employee. I didn't have to answer to her just because we'd known each other since high school, but frequently, I did. Usually I played the role of the mother, as well as the boss, having to censor what she looked like and what she wore to the office and counsel with her when her boyfriends dumped her.

She was correct, though. Today she did look normal. Normal hair color for a change, dishwater. Normal casual—if not office—attire, slacks and a blouse that actually matched, blues and browns. I'm disregarding the Crocs. All this doesn't take into account the mothering I had to do with Candy, our half-day high school helper. I really had to look after Candy and not just on isolated occasions.

"Hey, where's Candy this afternoon?" My cheek throbbed. I tried not to scrunch up my face as I continued the conversation.

Margaret headed toward the kitchen and said over her shoulder, "Went to the courthouse to pick up more papers to serve. Have you noticed how much that part of our business has grown?"

"Yeah, I did notice. That's what I was doing today. At the last one, I was mauled by a German Shepherd."

"Oh, Mavis." Margaret stopped halfway into the next room. "You're lucky you don't look any worse than you do."

"Thanks, I think."

"So, you want that BLT or not?"

"On stone-ground wheat with lots of mayo? Yes. Yes, I do. And a dill pickle on the side, please." My mouth watered. "I'll eat as soon as I get finished seeing our new client, who I assume is waiting for me in my office."

She clapped her fingers over her mouth, eyes wide. "Heck, I totally forgot. I gave her a cup of tea, though."

Well, that was something. I did an about face to go to my office.

"Oh, and Mavis, I interviewed her."

My stomach lurched but not from hunger. I reversed course again but had to stop myself from rushing to where she stood and strangling her. She knew better. She was under strict orders to usher them into my office, if they didn't want to sit in reception, and do nothing else.

Interviewing potential clients was not Margaret's job. She could work a computer like nobody I had ever known. She could find anything on the Internet. She could program our electronic gadgets while hardly referring to the instructions that came with them.

But Margaret came across to people who didn't know her as a—ah, not exactly an airhead, to use a cliché, or one beer short of a six-pack, to use another, and though I loved her dearly, I didn't want clients to judge me and my investigative business by anything Margaret said or didn't say. And I do not exaggerate.

So after I gave her the look, the one that communicated my unhappiness with her behavior, eyebrows drawn together, squinty eyes, pursed lips, I hurried toward the back of our little house-office. I hoped the potential client waited for me. I hoped the potential client hadn't had second thoughts and snuck out the door when no one was looking.

Margaret called after me in a fierce whisper, "You'll like this one, Mavis. It's another murder case. Someone chopped up her brother with an ax."

Chapter 2

HEAVING MY HIP AGAINST THE DOOR, which always stuck and needed to be adjusted, I shoved my way into my office. Sitting across from my desk, tapping something into her cell phone, was a small woman with short, curly, gray-streaked brown hair and pink-framed glasses. When I burst through the entrance, she made eye contact with me and held up a finger. While I side-stepped around my desk to my chair, she continued her tapping and wheezed each time she took a breath. More than a hint of rose scent filled the air.

Plopping into my chair, I waited to get her attention. She had high cheekbones, a button nose, and the thinnest of lips, pursed as though she held a cigarette in her mouth. Maybe she'd quit, like me. If she hadn't, with that wheezing, she should. Straightening some papers on my desk, I continued to wait until her attention shifted, which wouldn't be very long if I had anything to do with it. Moments later, she clicked a button on the side of her phone and laid it in her lap. "Isley Gibson," she said and reached across the desk.

"Mavis Davis."

She made short shrift of our handshake, her grasp firm, if perfunctory. Her eyes roved over my face and stopped at my injury.

"I apologize for being tardy." I touched my bandage. "I had to tidy myself up a bit after an incident with a dog."

Her face wrinkled up. "I hope you had a doctor tend to that."

"Later." Opening a drawer, I took out a legal pad on which I wrote her name. "So, Ms. Gibson, my assistant told me briefly about your brother. I'm so sorry for your loss. Is his death the reason you've come to see me?" I hoped my expression looked more sympathetic than curious.

She adjusted the cuffs on her fatigue-green jacket and scooted to the edge of her chair. The lens in her glasses magnified her eyes enough for me to see they were gray with a fleck of green. Pearl drop earrings dangled as she moved. She clasped her phone with one hand and gripped the edge of my desk with the other. "Yes, it certainly is," she said with perfect enunciation and no hint of a Southern accent. "They haven't caught the person responsible for his demise."

I wondered whether she had worked as a teacher. She sounded like one of the sixth-grade teachers at my elementary school. Nodding, I waited to hear her story.

"My brother, Skip Linden, lived in Galveston for most of his life after he graduated from the Academy."

"What academy?"

"Oh, sorry, the California Maritime Academy." She bobbed her head as though confirming her statement and followed that up with a wracking cough. My chest hurt just listening to her.

Under her brother's name, I wrote down the information as she told it to me. "So, he worked in the maritime industry out of Galveston?"

"Well, really, those people work all over, but when he became a cruise ship captain, he mostly worked out of Florida."

"Even though a lot of ships cruise out of Galveston?"

She swished her hand in the air. "Yes. Yes. Yes. That doesn't matter."

8

Okay. I'd follow her lead, let her tell her story in her own way. I think that's in the detective rule book somewhere, maybe number fifty-eight. "So…"

"He would fly back to Galveston when he had his leave. His cruise line didn't sail to Galveston, not that any really do, except, of course, the cruises that originate there. Anyway…" Still nodding.

"So, he lived here. Did he have a family? A beach house? What part of the island did he live in? What was his situation?" My foot involuntarily tapped on the plastic floor mat under my chair. I guess I'm not so good at letting people tell their stories their own way.

"I'm getting to that." She arched an eyebrow. "Don't rush me." She coughed again, this time not as badly.

"Yes, ma'am," I said, feeling as though I was under her command.

"He would be here—not in Houston, in Galveston—for varying lengths of time. Or so I understand from speaking to his family."

Just before I interrupted her again to ask for her contact information, I spotted a sheet of paper next to a glass of iced tea. Margaret had taken down Isley Gibson's name, address, and phone number already. Good girl. I took a sip of tea and watched her face as she spoke. She told me he had a wife, three children—the third one being a surprise—and a house on the west end of the island. I took down the address.

She said, "It was hard on the family, his being gone so much, but Roxanne said she knew he would be a ship's captain when they were married. They went together for a long time." Her face scrunched up as though she were thinking hard.

"Married when?"

Her forehead released, and her eyes lit up. "Thirty years ago, this month."

So, he was probably in his fifties. If they'd had the children in the first few years of their marriage, the kids would be grown and most likely had flown the coop.

Afraid of being too inquisitive, I kept my eyes on her and my

9

breath even. The side of my face throbbed. I tried not to squint at her, to let her see my pain, not wanting her to interpret it as dislike. I would go to one of those emergency care clinics after she left, at least to get something to help with the pain.

"Otherwise, they were a loving family."

"Otherwise?"

She pursed her lips. "When he was at home, in town. That's what Roxanne says."

"His wife." I was getting a little confused.

"Yes." Her words came out in a rush. "When the kids were little, he'd plan his time around their schedules, as much as anyone in that position could do, so he could spend time with them. He tried to attend their games, like Little League, and their other activities. He wanted as close a relationship with them as he could have for someone who traveled on the job." She coughed again and then again. "You have a tissue? I ran out while I was waiting for you."

I handed over the box and studied her while she spit out something. Clearly, she was ill. I could make an uneducated guess about what was wrong but would wait until the end of the interview. If she didn't tell me, I'd ask. The information could make a difference, though I wasn't sure yet what that could be. I was trying to be patient, though wanting her to cut to the chase, but the poor lady clearly couldn't control her coughing. Margaret would have to continue to hold that food for me. My stomach gurgled. I cleared my throat and took another swallow of tea. I've been accused of being callous, and often I am, I suppose, but my main thing right then was to get hired or not and then to eat. I've been told I'm not very likable when I'm hungry.

She blew out a short breath and followed that with a short inhale and looked at me. "I don't mean to belabor my explanation. I just want to make sure I'm thorough."

"Okay, no problem." My stomach growled, way louder than the gurgling.

"He did the same when they were older. I don't want you to think he was aloof when they became teenagers. He wasn't." She grabbed another tissue. "I'm not explaining it very well. I just want you to know he was really close to his family. Not just the kids, his wife too." She bit her lip. "Roxanne's been heartbroken since his death."

Finally, we're getting to the death. I licked my lips in anticipation of getting to the juicy—I mean—*important* part. I chanced another arched eyebrow. "Not to interrupt or anything, but how long ago did he meet his demise?"

"Five years—this month." Her eyebrows drew together. "Yes, he died the night of their anniversary. I thought you'd be wondering." She wiped her eyes. "It was the saddest thing." She sat up straight, shoulders back. "Anyway, I must stick to the business side of this, or I'll never get through it."

"All right. Just a moment. Let me catch up with my notes." My mind was racing with the possibilities. I scribbled a few things on my legal pad mostly to give myself a chance to think. Did I want to take a case in Galveston? Would the GPD get too bent out of shape if I looked into one of their stale cases? Would the client pay for a beach house for me to stay in while I was trying to figure this thing out, or would I have to drive back and forth fifty miles each way? She couldn't expect me to stay in Motel Whatever.

"The day he died, he was at home on vacation. You can ask Roxanne how long he was home for. I've forgotten." She scooted forward again, so close to the edge of the chair I feared she'd slip off. "From what I understand—because I wasn't here, I was in California—they had gone out to a very expensive restaurant and had a very expensive seafood dinner. They'd had a few drinks and had shared a bottle of champagne before they left home."

Now I was scribbling. "Guess I can get the name of the restaurant and all from the wife?"

She nodded. The muscle in her jaw flexed. "Then they went to an event at the opera house. I'm not sure, but I think when they returned home, they had sex. It was, after all, their anniversary."

"Of course." That would be the appropriate thing to do. "The kids were all grown by then? All living away from home?"

"Well, not exactly." She coughed again.

Not exactly? Hmmm.

"Their son and his wife and baby were staying with my brother at the time. My nephew had lost his job and couldn't find another one. His wife had a little job working as a substitute teacher but didn't make much."

"Were they home when Skip and Roxanne returned?"

"I think they'd gone to bed. It was pretty late for a couple with a baby to still be up."

"So then what happened?"

"Roxanne says they went to sleep. Then, she says, something woke her up. She wasn't sure what. She thought maybe John or Vonnie had come downstairs and gone into the kitchen for something."

"Two story house?"

"Yes, one of those ones up on, what do they call them, pilings? Stilts? A large, tall beach house up on stilts with several stories, way down toward the end of the island."

"Those cost a lot."

"Cruise ship captains do well, plus I think they had a pretty hefty mortgage. You can ask Roxanne."

"So, Roxanne will be available to me if I take this case? Does she know you're here? That you want to hire me?"

"Not exactly."

Again, not exactly. "What then, exactly?"

"Well, I told her I was going to hire someone to find out who killed him, but she said all she wanted to do was put it behind her and get on with her life."

"Can't blame her there after five years. She must have been living a nightmare."

She crossed her arms. "I don't care if she likes it or not. He was my brother, and I want to know who murdered him."

I reared back in my chair. "Okay. All right. I'm just wondering whether she'll cooperate with me if I take this case."

"You keep saying *if.*"

"You haven't hired me yet, Ms. Gibson. You don't even know what my rate is—my daily or hourly rate—and I charge expenses."

She rose up out of her seat and sat down again. "Yes, I do. Your assistant, Margaret, told me." The muscles in her jaw flexed again. She was one tense lady.

Margaret, again. Well, I didn't really mind. I hated talking about money. I just liked receiving it. "Well, then, if you'll finish telling me the basics, I'll let you know if I think I can be of any help."

She cleared her throat and spit something into a tissue again. "Okay, then. Well, Roxanne said after she heard the noise, she tried to go back to sleep, but then there was a noise in the room with them. She sat up in bed, and someone knocked her out."

I flinched. OMG. Poor lady. I pressed my lips together so tightly I'm sure they turned white. Isley was staring at me, her eyes hard, her face scrunched up, grim.

"Roxanne says when she woke up, there was blood everywhere, all over her. She thought at first she must be hurt but didn't feel hurt and reached out to Skip and put her hand in a crevice of blood."

Double OMG. Glad now I hadn't eaten. I swallowed, my throat dry. My glass was almost empty.

"She screamed and jumped out of bed and flipped on the light. Skip was dead, chopped up from the neck down, his eyes staring at the ceiling." Isley was breathing hard, wheezing. "I've been working up the nerve to tell this all at once, but it's really difficult."

"I'm sure it must be. I'm having a hard time hearing it. Just take your time." I wasn't as squeamish as I once was, but these facts could make anyone wince. "I'm sorry if you feel I've been rushing you."

Her eyes had welled up with tears. "She ran out the door to the stairs and yelled for the kids—John and Vonnie—and collapsed on the bottom step. They called the police, and there was an investigation. The police never figured out who did it."

We stared at each other for a few moments.

I weighed my next words carefully because who doesn't want a new client? "I understand you want to find out who the culprit or culprits were. Don't you think, though, that it's a little late?"

"I just want a fresh pair of eyes on this, Ms. Davis. If I don't get closure soon, I'll never get closure." She exhaled, her cheeks puffing out. "I've got the money to pay you, your daily rate like Margaret said, hourly, whatever you need. I cashed in my 401K. Of course, I'll pay your expenses too. If you find a reasonable place to stay in Galveston, I'd love for you to spend every day looking into my brother's case."

She had a lot of faith in me. More than I had in myself, especially with an old case like hers. "I can't promise you anything other than that I'll do my best. Will you be able to live with whatever I find out, even if it means your brother was into something unsavory?" Because my gut, still reeling from a vision of his hacked-up body, told me her brother had to have been involved in something serious.

"Well," she said with a big sigh, "I won't have to live with it very long. I have COPD."

Wincing, I said, "I wondered." Deep breath. "I'd just like to know one more thing before I agree to take your case. Is there a reason you chose me? My office? Did someone refer you or what?"

She studied my face, hers one of mild surprise. "I didn't want to use a Galveston investigator, so I went to the internet and did a search."

"There are larger firms. Way larger."

"I liked your web page. And someone put a comment on it, some man, about how good you were."

Well, blow me over. Margaret had said we needed a web page. I had told her to go for it. Last time I looked at it, I didn't see anything remarkable. Didn't see any comments. Guess I needed to look again. "Good to know."

"And I thought a female investigator would be good."

"Alright, then." I smiled just enough that it didn't hurt. "Let's get started. There are some more things I need to know, and then Margaret will go over the contract and all that with you."

"Okay." She cleared her throat and relaxed. "What else do you want me to tell you?"

"Did—do the police have any suspects at all?"

She shook her head. "Roxanne might know. I didn't ask her. She really shies away from talking about it."

"What do they have, if you know?"

She tore at the tissue in her hands. "According to Roxanne, a trail of blood out of the house and in the sand toward the water. An indication of a small boat being beached."

"You've obviously had a few conversations about it. Was that with Roxanne or the police? Are you staying with her? I mean, I imagine you must have had some heart-to-hearts."

Grim-faced, forehead wrinkled, she said, "Who said anything about me staying with her? I hardly know her."

"I thought you said she'd been married to your brother for thirty years when he died."

"She was, but I never met her until after he was killed." She actually said that without an ounce of emotion in her face.

I sat up straighter. What an interesting twist. "You never met her before he died? What about at their wedding?"

She shook her head again. "I didn't attend their wedding. I wasn't invited."

I dropped my pen and held my palm toward her. "Wait. Wait. Back up. You've left out a few things, don't you think?"

Her face softened before tightening up again. "I've told you everything you need to know, Ms. Davis. Can't you just get on with it?"

"I…don't…think…so." I raised my eyes and gave her what I thought of as my schoolmarm look—one she might have given to her class if she had been a teacher.

"Why does it matter what our relationship was?" She gritted her teeth.

"Did your parents go to the wedding?"

"They had died. Our grandmother wanted to go, but she was too frail. Not that Skip invited her, but I think he would have let her go if I'd pressed him. Not that he spoke to me. I guess if *she* had pressed him on it."

Her brother didn't speak to her. This was getting better and better. Ignoring my rumbling stomach, I continued to press *her*. "You and your brother weren't speaking when he got married?"

She drew a deep breath—deep for her—and coughed. When she was through and after she did the spitting thing again, she launched into an explanation. Her eyes rested on my face as she spoke. I tried not to react, which wasn't easy.

"About forty years or so ago, my brother and I got sideways about something. He stopped speaking to me. Wouldn't return my calls. Wouldn't answer my letters. I didn't know if it was something I'd said at our parents' funeral or what. He wouldn't say. Just disappeared out of my life." She jumped up and began pacing.

I made some notes and waited for her to continue. Every time she would sigh, she would cough. I don't think I have ever been as patient as I was that day.

"I tried to keep track of him, but after he graduated from the Academy, he moved around quite a bit before settling in Galveston. I moved around, too, so I was busy with my life."

"What did you do occupation-wise?"

She stopped. "I was in the army." She preened. "I was in the first graduating class of women from West Point."

"Impressive." No wonder she acted like she was issuing commands.

"Doesn't matter." She waved a hand at me. "So, he was moving around a lot, as was I. He was my only sibling, so I wanted a relationship with him. I couldn't understand what was going on."

"You never found out?"

"No. After a long time, I found Roxanne on Facebook, and she and I communicated a little, but that was it. Then when I saw he had died, I kept messaging her until she agreed to talk to me on the phone."

"And now you want to find out why he died?"

"Yes. And his family. I want to know whatever you can find out about them too."

"But you're friends with Roxanne on Facebook, so you know about her. I mean, she's letting you into her life now, right? I assume," I hate that word, "you've met her and been to her house now?"

"Yes, briefly, but her background—I mean, just if you can find out anything I might want to know." She folded her arms about herself and began walking around my office. Maybe she had to use the restroom. "Here's the thing, Mavis. I was planning on leaving my estate to Skip. I don't have anyone else."

"Even though—"

"Even though he wouldn't let me into his life. I knew he had kids. I want them to have whatever is left when I die, and the grandkids, however many there are, for college or whatnot. They're my only relatives." She stopped in front of my desk. "I want to be remembered. Is that so bad?"

Boy, howdy. My emotions were all over the place, but this wasn't about me. I studied her for a few minutes. "Why don't you sit back down, Ms. Gibson? I'm going to take your case, okay? Just a few more bits of information are all I need."

She sat and straightened her skirt and crossed her arms again. "At this point, there's nothing left to tell, but go ahead, shoot. What do you want to know?"

I leaned back and drew a breath. I knew this was going to be a hard one, but I'd agreed to take it, and I would. The question was, what other information was she hiding from me?

Chapter 3

I AGREED TO LOOK INTO CHARLES EDWARD (Skip) Linden's demise, for several reasons. First, I could use a trip to Galveston in the summer. In spite of the other tourists who would be jamming the seawall and the beaches, I wouldn't mind a swim in the Gulf of Mexico and sand between my toes. Second, Isley had money to pay me. That's always a good thing. Finally, Skip's murder had piqued my curiosity. Who carries around an ax to do someone in?

Isley and I spent a few more minutes together before I sent her to Margaret to sign a contract and turn over the money. Margaret enjoys collecting money and keeping our books. I've done it, but I find it awkward to look into someone's eyes and quote a dollar amount. I find it hard to believe someone would actually pay me to snoop about their private business. I've always had a curious mind and love the heck out of finding out interesting facts. Not to mention the blood and guts thing, and in Skip's case, a lot of guts, which, though it might make some people puke, drew me in. Morbid, yes; unhealthy, maybe, but I can't help it. I've always been fascinated by crime and motives and what goes on in people's brains.

Isley wasn't gone five minutes when Ben showed up, in the middle of the day, no less. "I'm taking you to the nearest clinic." He loomed in the doorway with one hand on the doorjamb and his other paw around my upper arm like he would a defendant's.

I had gone into the bathroom at the back of our little house-office and was studying my damaged face in the mirror when he appeared. He was dressed in his detective garb, to-wit: lightweight tan suit, light blue cotton shirt, loosened tie, and saddle brown wingtips.

Lieutenant Ben Sorenson of the Houston Police Department is, was, and probably always will be my long-time partner, unless he gets tired of my refusing to marry him and settle down. I don't know what it is about this tall, dark, and handsome man this sometime sexist, patronizing, and annoying personage, that keeps me with him and him with me, but it's like we're glued at the hip. His habits may be worse than other men's, but he's a fine person. I'm a big girl and can tolerate a little sexism and patronizing behavior. I call him on it every chance I get. I don't want children, at least not right now. I don't want to live with someone, either. I like sex. So does he. And we're both good at it. We have the perfect arrangement. He might spend the night occasionally, but I can always send him home. If I'm at his house, I can always go home. What's not to like?

"Margaret called you, didn't she? I'm going to kill her." I tried to wrench my arm away, but his grip was vise-like.

He turned my face toward his and winced. "Babe, if you don't get that treated, you could end up with a scar on your beautiful face."

Now how could any woman resist that? I would have grinned at him, but if my face had wrinkled on the one side, it would have been painful. "Okay, let me get my purse."

He accompanied me to my office. "I parked behind the office."

"Just give me a moment to assassinate Margaret, and then we can go." I handed him my purse and stalked to the front desk.

Margaret had to have heard me coming. She kept her back to me, her fingers continuing to tap something into the computer.

"You're grounded for life," I said to her back.

She didn't turn around. "Ha. You wish you were my mother."

"I'm letting him take me to a clinic, but don't think this is the end of the discussion."

The cowbell dangling above our front door clanged. We put it there so no one could sneak up on us. You never know who might walk in on you when you're not looking. In this case, it was Candy, our half-day high school worker.

"Shit, Mavis, what happened to you?" She wore her blue and green plaid school uniform and white blouse. Her hair, to my surprise, was more than a couple of shades pinker than my own—not to say mine is pink—it's red.

"How many times do I have to ask you not to use that language?" I shot her my best scowl without causing myself more pain.

"You do it." She slapped some papers onto the desk.

"We're not having this discussion right now. Anyway, what are you doing in your school uniform in the middle of summer?"

She did a little hop. "I figured no one would suspect me of being a process server if I looked like a student. Pretty smart, huh?"

Ever since she'd turned eighteen and gotten her driver's license and a clunker car, and I'd let her start serving documents, she'd thought up clever ways to disguise her intentions. Pride filled me at the genius of my young protégé, however I didn't let her see that very often. Didn't want it to go to her head. She had often come up with lame ideas as well.

"Yes, clever. Listen, Margaret has more work for you. I'm going to get my face seen by a doc." I turned toward her, so she could get the full effect.

Her face scrunched up, and she stepped back. "Eww, gross."

"Me and a dog had a disagreement." I gave her a what-can-you-do look. "Ben is taking me."

She bit into a cookie from a plate next to the computer. The aroma of chocolate filled the air. My stomach, which apparently wasn't satisfied with the two bites of the BLT I'd taken before Ben showed up, rebelled. I snatched a cookie too and took a big bite. OMG. My mouth watered. My stomach growled. "You're going to have to bake some more of these, Margaret. And wrap up my sandwich, please, for later. See y'all when I get back."

My trip to Galveston was delayed because of the length of time we'd spent at the emergency care clinic, all for one stitch in my cheek. We were there all afternoon and into the early evening. Margaret had stayed at the office in case I needed her, which is one of the reasons we got along so well. She wasn't then, and never was, *just* an employee. She and I were BFFs. I asked her when we returned from the clinic if she'd call down to Galveston and see if she could find me a place to stay while I packed up my things. Ben came inside with me and plunked down in one of my client chairs. I had a feeling he was hoping for some action that night. I wouldn't mind some myself.

"Ben, don't you have an acquaintance or two on the force at the Galveston Police Department?" I had grabbed a tote bag and my roller bag, opening both so I could pitch things in them.

"I know a couple of men at the Sheriff's Office who used to be at the PD." He picked up a magazine and started thumbing through it. His voice changed, taking on his third-degree tone. "Why?"

"Just wondering." I walked around my desk and patted his arm. "Thanks for caring for me this afternoon. I don't know how you managed to take off half a day, but I appreciate it." He was used to me brown-nosing him and didn't let it affect him most of the time.

"Half a sick day. Have a ton of them." He grabbed my hand and pulled me to him. "You know I'm always at your service, ma'am."

I leaned down and gave him a peck on the mouth, hoping he'd let go so I could get packing. "So, does that mean you'll give me the names of the guys you know at the Galveston County Sheriff's Office?" I pulled at my hand, but he held onto it, trying to coax me onto his lap. He must be hot to trot but not now, not ever, would I have sex in my office. Especially with Margaret still there.

"Was that woman I walked by earlier in your office from Galveston?" He patted his leg, wanting me to sit down.

I laughed. "She's from California." I tried to take my hand back. "You have to let go of me if I'm going to get this done. We can go to my house after dinner."

He released me. "She didn't hire you for a case in California, did she?" His voice held a lot of skepticism.

Would it be so impossible for someone to come here to hire me to go to California? Well, yeah. The chance of that was about the same as winning the lottery. "No, she didn't."

"She did hire you, though." His voice gave away his desire to know what I was hired for. He only wished he could have some say-so over my cases. That was never going to happen.

"None of your business. If she did, that would be confidential." I decided against the tote bag and threw it on the credenza. I put my laptop in the roller bag along with a camera, though mostly these days I used my cell phone for pictures.

He crossed his arms. "I know she did because she went with Margaret after she left your office. And Margaret takes care of the business side of things."

"Okay. But we've been over this many times. Please don't ask me to disclose any information about the case to you." I headed for the door, to go to the safe. "Will you give me your friends' names and contact info or not?"

"I don't like it, but yeah. I'll email them. Where are you going?"

"To get my .38. You don't think I'm going down there without any way of protecting myself, do you?"

He jumped up. "You don't need your gun. You don't even know anything about the case yet." He caught up with me and grabbed my arm.

"Look, I agreed to keep it in the safe when I'm in the office, but I'm not going down there defenseless." I stared up at him, my hands on my hips. "And besides, I do so know what the case is about, and I'm taking my gun." I started for the safe again.

"What can I say to persuade you to leave it here? You can always come back for it if someone threatens you, but hell, no one down there even knows about you yet."

"I'll never understand you, Ben. You carry a gun." A bit of anger had started to burn in my stomach.

The muscle in his jaw flexed. "I'm a cop. I'm required to carry it twenty-four-seven, and you know it."

I stood there staring at him for a moment. If I didn't give in, he'd keep up the argument all night. If I did give in, I'd have peace. I could always come back and get it later. I figured I'd come back to the office every few days anyway, just to check on things. "Okay. But I just don't see the difference between me and a female police officer. You know I can hit the target when I shoot it."

"Shooting at people and at targets are two different things. So, you won't take it?"

"Not now." I cocked my head and frowned up at him.

"Don't give up on me. I'm trying to move into the twenty-first century. I just don't see why you need it yet and just taking it to have it, well, too many people do that these days." He grinned. "I worry about you." He gave me one of his sexiest looks and flashed his eyebrows in an effort to make me laugh. "Want to go to dinner now?"

I shook my head and traipsed back into my office to finish up.

"Just have a few more things to get. Wish I'd had time to make a list. Why don't you go run an errand or something, and I'll meet you at the restaurant? I have a bit of research I want to do before I leave."

He gave me a look that said he was suspicious. I knew he thought I'd go to the safe as soon as he left, but that wasn't it. I wanted to look up the case and get some information before I went to Galveston. "And I'll have time to find out whatever background I can before I go down there."

"You're not going to get your .38 as soon as I leave, are you?"

"No. I promise."

"And you're really not going to tell me anything?"

"Just that it's an old case, so the PD shouldn't get too pissed off about it if I poke around."

"You hope."

"Yes, I hope. And I promise if I get in a jam, I'll call you, even though you know good and well I can take care of myself."

He cleared his throat, but I didn't take the bait. "Okay, so what I'm going to do is get Chinese and meet you at your house in forty-five minutes." He tapped his watch to be sure to get my attention. "Forty-five minutes."

"I heard you. Now go." I followed him to the back door, closing and locking it behind him. Then I pulled my laptop out of my roller bag and opened it for the first time in quite a while. I'm somewhat computer savvy but not fond of the Internet. I would let Margaret do everything if there were time, but Isley wanted me to get on down to Galveston as soon as I could.

The website for the Galveston Police Department required me to put in contact info in order to ask for information. I didn't want to do that yet, so I shut that page down. The newspapers in the county had archives. That was more to my liking. I didn't have to identify myself. I spent the next few minutes searching and found what I was looking for. Of course, if I wanted more than the initial article, I was invited to pay an annual fee, which I wasn't ready to do either. I really just wanted to find out where I needed to go to find information. Once I was settled, I'd dive in for more, like the name of the reporter and the investigating officer. At the very least, I'd find the name of the reporter who would be able to tell me the name of the investigating officer. Not that I necessarily believed the investigating officer would talk to me, but there was always a chance. This is what I found:

SHIP CAPTAIN SLAIN

Police are investigating the apparent murder of a cruise ship captain at a beach house on Galveston's West End on Friday night. Authorities say that at 2:00 a.m., they were called to the home of Captain Charles Edward Linden by his wife, Roxanne Linden. The couple, their son, daughter-in-law, and grandchild, lived in a multi-story, high-raised beach house in an exclusive subdivision fronting the Gulf of Mexico. Sometime after midnight, the assailant or assailants entered the home, knocked out Mrs. Linden and proceeded to kill Captain Linden. Authorities are not aware of the motivation for the crime but are not ruling out the possibility of transportation of drugs or other

...See SLAIN A3

I printed out the bit of the article I could see and the home page of the archives and tucked them in my tote bag along with my laptop and cables. By that time, it was well after the time I was supposed to meet Ben. Margaret had been able to locate a condo in which I could stay for a week with check-in the next afternoon and check-out the following Friday by ten. The location was at the end of the Galveston seawall, which I hoped would be convenient in light of what I assumed would be tourist traffic dominating the roadways.

Ben and I spent Thursday night together. I put discussion of the case on the off-limits list. I packed. We made love. And Friday morning found me on the Gulf Freeway with adrenaline surging through my chest the way it always does in anticipation of a new adventure. I hoped Galveston was ready for me.

Chapter 4

THE CONDO MARGARET RENTED FOR ME was not at the end of the seawall. It was past the end of the seawall. If there had been a hurricane in the Gulf of Mexico, I never would have unpacked my bag. But there wasn't. So, I did. A coating of salt covered the window that faced the gulf. The smell of seaweed drifted in from the beach. The temperature with the heat index had to be over a hundred. I was never so glad air conditioning had been invented before I'd been born.

After emptying my suitcase, I climbed back into my Mustang and headed farther west, down the island, and farther and farther until I thought I'd run out of island. Finally, I arrived at the quote unquote *subdivision* where the Lindens lived. If it hadn't been for the navigation system in my cell phone, I'd have been driving up and down that rural road for the rest of my life.

Ginormous, high-raised houses facing the water ran parallel to the road, showing just how desperate people are to have a piece of the beach—a piece facing the water. Finding the exact house was another matter. The owners must have agreed to hide the house numbers as a form of security because I couldn't find the address. My GPS had said, "Arrived at your destination," when I drove onto the tiny bit of paving that pretended to be a street running beside the row of houses. So, I drove to the end and parked. Before I set out, I ditched the blouse I wore as a faux jacket over my T-shirt. If there hadn't been a Gulf breeze, I would have felt the humidity worse than in Houston.

At the first house, the door to the elevator was locked, so I climbed the stairs to what I assumed was the front door, which was wood-framed with rectangular double-paned, obscured glass with a Texas star in the middle. I was as impressed and as much in awe as I had been when I'd investigated another case where the people had money, the one that had taken me to River Oaks in Houston. When I arrived at the top step and caught my breath, I cursed the locked door to the elevator down below. Piss ants.

I jammed my thumb on the doorbell about five-jillion times. The chimes rang in the distance. No one answered. The second house was locked up tight as well. And the third. I walked back to the end of the road and retrieved my vehicle and drove to the fourth. The fourth had a coffee table and a bookshelf sitting next to the locked elevator door on the slab under the house. Upstairs, I banged on their door. No one answered, but as I turned to leave, a woman dressed in a man's plaid sport shirt over black leggings came out onto the deck that encircled the fifth house and leaned against the maple-colored wooden railing. The houses were close enough together that she was in hearing distance.

"Hey," I called to her. "Good morning."

"Good morning," she said back. She opened the door, and a German Shepherd came bounding out.

OMG. Not again. "No need to sic your dog on me, ma'am. I'm merely looking for the Linden family. I guess, really, it's just Mrs. Linden now?" I grinned, hoping she could see I was as harmless as a sea slug.

She took hold of the dog's collar. "She moved."

I caught my breath. Moved and left the furniture down by the elevator? I hadn't had time to look through any of the windows. "When was that, ma'am, if you don't mind?"

"Yesterday." She pulled a pair of sunglasses out of her shirt pocket and put them on.

Darn. My unlucky day. If I'd just come on down the day before, I could have caught the Widow Linden. Staring from the neighbor to the dog for a moment, I wondered if she'd answer a few questions. No time like the present to find out. "Do you know Mrs. Linden?"

"Met her a few times." The dog pulled back, trying to get loose.

"Have you lived here very long? Well, I guess what I want to know is how long have you lived here?"

"We bought this place two years ago when I retired." She tilted her head. "Why're you looking for Mrs. Linden?"

"So, you live here full time?" Maybe she knew the neighbors. Maybe some of the neighbors had lived there back when the murder took place.

"My husband commutes to Houston to work. He goes in on Mondays and returns on Fridays. A lot of people with houses out here do that. Some only come down on the weekends."

Talkative. That was good. "What about the folks down toward the end?" I pointed to the three houses I'd been to and moved to the railing around the former Linden house.

"Weekend people."

I nodded. "And the ones on the other side of you?"

"The one next to the end is full time. He goes into Houston sometimes and stays at an apartment if he has business or wants to go to the theater or whatever. The others are weekenders and sometimes they rent their places out. So why did you say you're looking for Rebecca?"

"Roxanne."

"Yes, Roxanne." She nodded. "We're not close friends."

Didn't sound like they were friends at all. "If you didn't live here five years ago, you probably don't know about the murder that took place here."

"Ha! Everyone knows about that. The realtors tell people when you look at houses. Warn them. Alert them. Whatever you call it. So, we can't come back and complain we weren't told when we bought a house nearby."

"Well, that's what I'm looking into."

"A stale case like that? Good luck. Where are you from?"

Her use of the word *stale* piqued my interest. Kind of a word used in the legal community. "Houston. Were you a police officer?"

"Court reporter for thirty years. Anyway, I don't know anything about it. Sorry." She yanked on the dog's collar and reached for her doorknob. "Frisky, sit." The dog sat.

"Do you mind telling me your name?"

"Smith."

Sure. "Uh..."

"Lauren. And yours?"

"Mavis Davis."

She smiled big enough that I knew she was trying not to laugh. "I wish I could help you. I love a good mystery."

"It is a tall order. Well, I guess I ought to knock on the other doors."

"Don't waste your time. Nobody is home at any of the other houses."

"What about that man you mentioned?"

"He goes to the mountains in Mexico for a few months each summer. It's cooler. Speaking of which, if you don't mind, I'm dying out here."

"Me, too. Thanks for speaking with me, Ms. Smith."

"Lauren. I wish I could be more help. I don't have anything much to do so if you need something..."

"I don't suppose you know where Mrs. Linden moved to?"

She shook her head and reached for the doorknob. "Sorry. I'm here every day." Her eyes bright, her eyebrows raised, she looked hopeful, like she wanted to help. "Give me a holler if I can do anything for you." She recited her number, which I immediately began to repeat to myself. "Or stop back by whenever you want."

Like I'd be in the neighborhood and drop in? I don't think so. But I kept repeating the number just in case. After she went inside, I glanced into Mrs. Linden's windows. Two large pieces of furniture sat close to the door, but the rest of the place was empty as far as I could tell. I ambled down the stairs and back to my car, perspiration trickling down my back. When I got inside, I started the car to get the air-conditioning going and swallowed a long drink of water from the bottle in the console. Her phone number I tapped into the little note pad app on my cell phone. Next stop, the library, to see if I could find further information on the murder.

Turning my Mustang around, I moseyed out of the small subdivision onto the farm-to-market road and launched my Mustang onto the asphalt after a group of speeding cars heading east toward the city. I hadn't gone half a mile when a moving van passed me going the other way. Could it be going to the Linden house for the last load of furniture? The only way to find out was to make a U-turn and follow it. And if it was, I could wait and follow it to the new house. Maybe I wasn't so down on my luck after all.

Turns out, I was correct in my assumption that the moving truck was returning to pick up the rest of Mrs. Linden's furnishings. Parking in the large lot of a realtor's office across from the alleged subdivision, I pointed my car toward the row of houses and waited with the engine running. No way would I suffer the Galveston heat for heaven knows how long. I could end up dead, steamed like a blue crab in a pot.

Fortunately, though, I didn't have to wait very long. The two guys who jumped out of the truck didn't waste any time clearing out the remaining furniture. When they pulled behind a pack of cars coming from down the island at warp speed, even though I was delayed by the next bunch, the size of the truck enabled me to follow with no problem. I tailed them up onto the seawall, which is miles of an urban park that keeps the Gulf of Mexico at bay during hurricanes. Traffic slowed. For seven or eight miles, we passed fishing piers, rock groins, families carrying folded chairs and ice chests down onto the sand, waves breaking on the shore, grocery stores, and hotels, until we turned off somewhere in the middle of the island. The truck stopped in front of a one-story home in a well-tended, older neighborhood with clipped lawns, wide and tall ginger plants, bougainvillea, and palm trees.

The guys immediately popped open the back of the truck and began unloading. I parked across the street and watched as they opened an unlocked door and carried the furniture inside. I waited. When they were through, they drove away. So, there I was, at lunch time, hungry again, and no sign of anyone at said house. All right, first knock on the door, meet her if she is inside, and then eat? Or eat, return, and then meet her? That was the gist of the conversation with my stomach. Thinking about the number of hungry tourists carousing on the island made me realize it would behoove me to eat later, rather than sooner.

Colorful tropical plants and herbs bookended Roxanne Linden's front steps, all two of them, and spread across the yard in front of the red brick and concrete porch. Two rocking chairs, one in front of each tall sparkling window, and a welcome mat in two languages, framed the storm door. Something swirled around in my stomach just before I pushed the doorbell. I hoped it was butterflies, not breakfast. I'm always a bit apprehensive right before I meet the first witness to a crime.

She answered right away. Roxanne was a petite, curly-haired brunette in her mid-fifties. She held a box cutter in one hand, the blade pointed right at my face. Lovely.

"Can I help you?" Her expression was not welcoming. No smile.

I cleared my throat. I towered over her. I'm not particularly intimidating, I don't think, but some short people don't like to be confronted by tall people. She took a step back.

"Hi. My name is Mavis Davis. I'd like to speak with you for a few minutes if you don't mind."

One eyebrow lifted. "About what? Are you selling something? Because I just moved here. I'm unpacking and don't really think I need anything right now."

"No, ma'am." I cleared my throat again. "You know Isley Gibson?"

"Oh, no." She folded her arms about her chest, the box cutter pointed more toward my throat than my face.

"Yes, ma'am." I drew a deep breath. "I'm a private investigator, and Isley hired me. I'm sure you know what for." I glanced past her. The house wasn't large but looked solid. Wood floors. Old-fashioned archway from the living room to what I guessed was the dining room. Kitchen on the far side of that. To the right, a hallway I figured led to the bedrooms and bathrooms.

She reached for the edge of her front door, a look of determination about her mouth, a muscle in her jaw working.

"Please don't do that, Mrs. Linden. I promise I won't be long, but if you shut me out, I'll never get all the facts I need to find out what happened to your husband."

She stared up at me for a moment or two, sighed, and opened the door wider. "All right. But you're going to have to help me open boxes while we talk." She held the box cutter toward me like one would the butt of a revolver. "I just moved, and I've got tons of stuff to do."

I took the box cutter. "Yes, ma'am. Where do you want me to start?" Stacks of boxes from a well-known office supply store were heaped everywhere, wide strapping tape keeping them closed. No used liquor or grocery store boxes for her. The tart aroma of vinegar came from the kitchen.

A muscle worked in her jaw. "How about the ones stacked in front of the couch? As soon as you get those done, you can sit down."

Walking to the sofa, I said, "This is a lovely neighborhood. Looks old and well-established."

"Some of the houses were built in the 1920s. Not this one, though. This one was a few years later. I like them because they're built solidly, not like new houses. And this neighborhood has never flooded in a hurricane."

I slashed the tape on the top box and ripped it open. "Way different from living on the beach."

She stopped what she was doing and said, "How did you know I lived down the island?"

"Uh, oh, Isley gave me the address, and when you weren't there, I followed the moving truck."

"Very clever of you." Her lips had thinned.

"Thanks." I braced myself and picked up the quite heavy box. "Where do you want me to put this?"

"What's in it? Did you look?"

"Oh." I put it down again and opened it. "Books and knick knacks." No wonder it was heavy.

"You can set it down over there against the wall." She pointed to about the only empty space in the room. "That's where my bookcases will go."

I lugged it over and set it down. "I wanted to ask you about your husband's demise."

"Demise. That's one way of putting it." She had produced some scissors from somewhere and was cutting through the tape on a box. She leaned down and took one scissor blade and swiped at the end of each box under the first one. "What did Isley tell you?"

"Just what you told her." I cut open another box. "I don't want to make this any harder on you than it has to be, Mrs. Linden. If you wouldn't mind just running through that night with me."

"You can call me Roxanne, Mavis. I've recited the facts so many times . . . " She glanced at me, frowning. "I guess it won't hurt for me to repeat the facts once again. Maybe then Isley will be satisfied that everything has been done that can be done."

"I appreciate that, Roxanne. I'll be putting everything in a report to her."

She put the scissors into the back pocket of her jeans and ripped the box open, stopping for a moment to make eye contact. "Skip and I had returned home from celebrating our anniversary. John—that's our son—and his wife, Vonnie, and their baby were staying with us temporarily. They were in the living room watching TV and went up to bed when we got home."

"Was that a problem for you?"

"Not at all. I liked having the company. My husband was gone so much."

I worked open the next box. More books. I again crossed the room and put the box next to the first one. I might have to ice my back later.

She peeked into a box and closed it again. "They had a small TV in their room. We didn't like them watching TV downstairs next to our bedroom—it was on the ground floor, so to speak." She carried the box down the hall to the first room on the right and returned. "I can't sleep if there's a lot of noise, so the rule was for them to go upstairs when we were going to bed, so we said our goodnights." She bent over to the next box and slit the tape with the scissors.

I crouched down and sliced into the third one in my stack, which was on the floor. "And then what happened?"

"Well, we went to bed." She wouldn't look at me.

"That's all?"

"You need the intimate details? It was our anniversary." She shifted her eyes. "I mean, you know how it is."

I didn't reply. I'd never had an anniversary.

She stood and put her hands on her hips. "Okay, we had sex. We always had sex on our anniversary. Skip had made that plain the first year we were married." She frowned. "Never did know what that was about. Maybe that's what his parents did. I don't know." Her demeanor and a look said, *Are you satisfied now?*

"So, then you went to sleep?" The third box held crystal candle holders and red candlesticks.

"We cleaned up and then went to sleep. Of course, we had a master bath downstairs in our bedroom. You haven't been inside the house, I take it, but you've seen it. You can imagine how nice it was inside, I'm sure."

Yeah, I was sure too. I wanted to get inside the house just to study the layout. "Yes, ma'am."

"Please don't *ma'am* me. I know it's a southern thing, but I don't like it. Makes me feel old."

"Okay. You were saying, y'all went to bed and then what?"

"Something woke me up. I heard noises. At first, I thought one of the kids had come downstairs for something, but then it sounded like someone was in the room with us. After that, I don't remember anything except a moment of pain." She stood and squared her shoulders and let out a huge breath. Her face had drawn up into a deep frown.

"And then?"

"And I don't know how long later, but I woke up with my head pounding. I thought I had gotten a migraine headache from the wine we drank. Sometimes that happens though I didn't drink very much." Her shoulders hunched, and her lips pressed together. She touched her forehead like she had a headache right then.

I stopped what I was doing and stood there, giving her a moment.

Her eyes came to rest on mine. Her shoulders dropped. In a whisper she said, "I didn't hear Skip's breathing machine—you know, CPAP machine—so I reached over to touch him and felt something wet." Her face blanched. "I moved my fingers a little and everything felt sticky and wet. When I turned on the bedside lamp, my hand was covered with blood. Skip's body was covered with blood. Blood was everywhere." As she spoke, her eyes grew wide and large. She reached out her hand to me.

I squeezed her hand and dropped it. A slight pain pulsed in my esophagus. I released a breath. "Could I have a drink of water?"

"What?" She shook her head as though clearing it—clearing away the memory. "Of course."

While she stepped into the kitchen, I blew out another puff of air. Interviewing her turned out to be tougher than I had imagined. She returned with the glass of water and stood still while I guzzled it. I handed it back to her. "Where do you want the candle holders and candle sticks?"

Her brow wrinkled again. "What? Oh. Bring the box in here to the kitchen, if you don't mind."

Following her into the kitchen, I set the box on the dinette table where she had pointed. We walked back into the living room together. "You weren't injured, right? And you saw no sign of anyone."

She nodded. "I ran to the staircase leading upstairs. Ran screaming, I'm told because I don't really remember that part. My son came downstairs. Vonnie wasn't far behind. I remember finding myself sitting on the bottom step." Her eyes glazed over like she was in a trance. "And then John, who must have gone into the bedroom, returned to where I was. He was hollering something. He stopped Vonnie from going into our bedroom. He said something to her. Something about Skip being dead." Her eyes searched my face. "He said, 'Call the police. Find a cell phone, and call the police.' He had some blood on him, too, but not much. Not like the spots on my arms and the blood covering my hand. I looked down and saw some on my nightgown. I think he must have touched his father like I did." She stopped and shook her head and stared up at me.

Whoa. I couldn't find my words for a moment. I went over to another box and stood staring at it, having a hard time focusing.

Finally, I cut it open. More books. I carried it to the others. Roxanne had resumed opening boxes as well.

"Roxanne, Isley tells me the police have never solved your husband's murder. Of course, that's why she hired me." I probably deserved a smack on the forehead for that one. Why else would I be there? "After all these years, have you come up with any idea who could have done such a horrible thing? I hate to sound insensitive, but could he have been involved with some illicit things like drugs or smuggling—I guess he went places as a cruise ship captain where he could have gotten ahold of something that could be smuggled, right?" Diamonds? Drugs? But I didn't say that.

She sat down on the floor and crossed her legs in what we used to call Indian-style—maybe now Native American-style? Anyway...

Looking up at me again, she shook her head. "I swear I've thought and thought. I guess he could have made some enemies along the way, but he never spoke to me about any."

"Hmm, well I didn't think this would be easy."

"What?" She continued sitting on the floor.

"I guess I was thinking aloud. Did he always get along with everyone as far as you know?"

"I worried for a long time that he'd done something that would make people hate him—us. I prayed someone wouldn't come after the rest of the family. If they were going to, I guess they would've done it by now."

"What has happened to the rest of the family? Like John, he's your oldest? Where is he now?"

"Ha. That's a good one. And no, he's the middle child. Maybe that's his problem." She began taking CDs out of the box she'd just opened and stacking them on the floor.

"He no longer lives with you?"

"He and Vonnie split up. Got a divorce." Her voice deepened. "I haven't seen my grandchild in a very long time."

"What about your son?"

"John is pretty much homeless. He started doing drugs after Vonnie left, and I kicked him out. Last I heard, he was moving from friend-to-friend, sleeping on their couches."

"And your other children?"

"Chuck is the only one who stayed local. In fact, he lives two blocks from here." She smiled for the first time, like she had known he was one child she'd have a relationship with. "Hanna Beth lives in Seattle."

About as far away as she could and still be in this country. I wondered why. What had taken her there? "What does she do for a living?"

"She's a vegan, a health nut. Runs a health food store." She licked her lips and sniffed.

"Would you mind giving me their contact information?"

"I guess not. Except for Vonnie's. You'll have to get that from John, if you find him. I can give you the name of one of his friends. He may know where John is."

"Thank you. And what about you? Have you built yourself a life since—since your husband passed away?"

She rolled her shoulders back and craned her head to look at me. I perched on the little bit of the sofa that was available.

"I'm trying. The insurance company gave me a hard time about paying. I about went broke trying to keep up that house. It took a long time to find a buyer. You don't know how repelled people can be when they know a murder—a gruesome one at that—took place in the master bedroom."

"I can imagine." My stomach, which had been quiet for some unknown reason, rumbled. "Excuse me. I haven't had lunch."

She nodded. "Anyway, the insurance company finally paid up last year. I had sold my husband's car and spent our savings paying for insurance and taxes and other costs on the house. Windstorm, hail, flood. You wouldn't believe. We'd paid off the mortgage, but beach houses require a lot of upkeep. The cleaning service charged me more than a hundred every time they showed up even for a couple of hours, and the house wasn't that dirty with only me in it." She got up and dusted herself off. "I could only find part-time work. I had been out of the job market for so long. My job barely paid for food and gas."

"And now?"

"What's left of his life insurance and the sale proceeds will take care of me for a long time. I paid cash for this house, and the bills will be a lot lower. It's solid and small—only two bedrooms. I should be good to go for quite a while." She hustled to a box that sat on the floor at the edge of the hall. The flaps were already open. She dug around inside and came up with a photo. "Here." Her hand shook. "This is Skip. You might need it."

The atmosphere in the room had changed. I didn't know why. "I was going to ask you, so thanks." Skip was in his ship's captain uniform and held his hat under one arm. Not a bad looking man. Thinning blond hair. Bushy eyebrows. Blue eyes. Tanned.

"Come into the kitchen, and I'll get the kids' contact information." Her movements had sped up. She didn't run, wasn't obviously hurrying, but definitely moved faster than she had for the previous half hour or so. She pulled a cell phone out of her purse, which sat on the end of the counter. "I can share them with you. What's your email address?"

"I'm so sorry. Let me give you a card." I dug into my own purse's side pocket and found one. When she reached for it, her hand was still shaking. We stood in the kitchen while she punched in the information. The kitchen had been updated, the appliances were way newer than last century. The kitchen wasn't overly elaborate. The appliances were mostly from Sears, so maybe it hadn't been Roxanne who'd updated it. She'd sounded like she could afford fancier ones now that the insurance had paid off. My cell dinged when the email landed.

"That's it. John's friend is the last one on the list." She put her hand on my elbow and guided me to the door.

Was I being given the bum's rush, albeit gentle, all of a sudden? "Well, thank you for meeting with me in the middle of your move."

Roxanne opened the front door and stepped forward to open the storm door too. "Mavis, would you keep in touch? Will you let me know what you find out?"

"Be glad to. And if you think of anything I might want to know, you have my card."

"Take care now," Roxanne said. She looked up and down the street and was closing the door when I glanced over my shoulder on the way to my car.

I climbed inside and turned the car air conditioner to full speed ahead. Just as I pulled away from the curb, a small yellow sports car—a BMW from the looks of it—parked at the curb. Who would buy a yellow BMW? I didn't even know they made them in that color. Anyway, as I drove by, a man jumped out with the key fob in his hand. The car chirped. He was about medium height, rubbery-looking body, gray hair, and a face like a platypus—ugly as homemade soap. I slowed and visually followed him as he raced to the front door of Roxanne's house and went in without knocking, ringing the doorbell, or using a key.

Chapter 5

'**M A SEAFOOD FREAK, SO I** had a hard time deciding which restaurant recommended by the "Best of Galveston Survey" to go to for lunch but headed downtown since I needed to be there anyway. I found several choices, ending up at one on the water, situated right next to a cruise ship terminal. When I entered, the smell of garlic and grilled fish caused an outcry from my stomach. *Feed me.* My table overlooked the beautiful Tall Ship Elissa, a barque, which I learned from the waiter means, "What kind of sails she has." Across the water on Pelican Island, stood an oil rig in for repairs. The sun reflected off the water. Small waves lapped against the pilings holding up the restaurant. For a moment, I wished Ben had been there with me.

Knowing Isley would reimburse me, I ordered the Gulf Red Snapper. I'd had a hard morning and needed to be rewarded. At least that's what I would tell Isley. It wasn't easy hearing about blood and guts.

Afterward, my GPS took me to the Rosenberg Library, which was less than five minutes away. Outside on one of the main streets, from Broadway to the wharves, is a huge statue of a bearded man sitting in a chair. Henry Rosenberg, I learned, the library's benefactor. From the

45

outside, half the library looked really old, and the other half looked new. It seemed to me to be a really nice-sized library for a city as small as Galveston. I was hoping it was modern enough to have a newspaper archives I could look through.

When I went inside, I was directed to the third floor, which housed a large number of computers that I could use to search the local newspaper's archives. I didn't even have to have a library card. Could it get any easier? Isley could have done some of this work herself, if she'd been so inclined. I wondered why she hadn't. In my purse, I had the article I'd printed out on Thursday. I used it for a reference point and found the second half of that story.

SLAIN *Continued A1*

motives. Captain Linden was employed as a cruise line ship captain, his home base Miami, Florida. He and his wife had made their home in Galveston for several decades and raised their children here. Police declined to state how the victim met his death, saying more would be revealed after an autopsy has been performed.

Like they needed an autopsy to know how he died? Probably just a formality and probably just telling the public what they wanted them to know. Some people might get squeamish at the idea that someone was running around the island and chopping up people with an ax, so that article was no help. I searched further. In the following day's paper, I found:

No Clues in Captain's Murder

Police are continuing to investigate the murder of Captain Charles Edward (Skip) Linden of Sandbar Beach, Galveston, who was found dead in his bedroom by his wife of thirty years. The circumstances around his death are not completely clear the police chief said. So far there are no suspects. The perpetrators are believed to have come to the home by boat. The medical examiner's office has not yet released a cause of death.

Well, that was no help either. I wondered if any other articles I found would be more of the same. If the cops knew anything, they weren't saying, but why hadn't a reporter sniffed it out?

The next article, which I found in the back of an edition a few days later, didn't reveal much either.

Captain's Death Still Unsolved

Autopsy results in the murder case of Captain Charles (Skip) Edward Linden reveal the victim was attacked with a sharp instrument which caused several wounds to the chest and abdomen. Police have no suspects at this time and are unsure of a motive. Captain Linden lived at Sandbar Beach with his wife. He was found dead last week at two a.m.

You bet it was a sharp instrument. Wouldn't a good reporter query further? Having decided I was wasting my time with newspaper articles, I printed what I'd found and got out of there. Next stop was the police station, which I discovered was back in the other direction. I headed down the tree-lined street of Broadway, which was also Interstate 45, for about thirty blocks and arrived at the Galveston Police Department, which was next to what they called the Justice Center. The buildings were relatively modern for an old city like Galveston. Police cars and some huge military-type vehicles I could only guess had been provided by Homeland Security sat to one side. The far side was covered by acreage of overgrown weeds. A train heading toward downtown ran down a track on the other side of the weeds.

Parking in front of the station, I walked inside and found a wide lobby with a few metal benches and a female officer in full police officer regalia sitting behind what had to be bullet-proof glass with one of those speaker thingies centered in it. There was a door on each side, to the right and to the left. I had been to Galveston years before. By before, I mean before that building and had been able to pretty much walk into the police station and talk to people person-to-person and overhear conversations from workstations and smell the coffee and burning cigarettes. This new place was quiet and sterile and scent-free.

I waited in line behind two other people, one of whom was clearly there on personal business. I couldn't help but hear the woman behind the glass instructing the young woman speaking through the glass on what to pick up at the grocery store. After a couple of minutes, the young woman moved aside. The next person wanted information on how to register a bicycle.

When it came my turn, I stepped up to the window and said, "Hello. My name is Mavis Davis. I'm a PI from Houston. I'd like to speak to someone about a murder case that occurred here in Galveston five years ago."

The woman behind the glass would have made a good poker player what with the deadpan look she gave me. She reached over a huge metal instrument panel and pressed a button on some kind of fancy intercom, spoke into it something that sounded like muffled Greek, and then said, "Have a seat. Someone will be with you in just a minute."

That minute turned into at least half an hour, which I filled by checking my emails and playing solitaire on my phone. Eventually a buzzer buzzed, and a huge and very tall cop came out of the door to the right of the window. He was uniformed and wore discolored black running shoes. He had a trim haircut, dark brown eyes, and a wide frown. I stood, and he walked right up to me, even into my personal space. That didn't bode well.

"Now, what can I do for you, ma'am?" He towered over me even more than Ben. I'd wager a guess he stood at least six-five. And smelled rancid, like he must have been out in the humid, Galveston heat earlier in the day.

I took a step back, so I could see him more easily. "My name is Mavis Davis. And you are?"

"Sergeant Fields." He pointed to the patch of stripes on his sleeve. "You're wanting some information about a murder case?"

"I'm not trying to interfere with an open investigation or anything. This case is five years old." That statement made no difference to his expression. "It's the Captain Linden murder. The one with an ax?"

His face screwed up. He hooked his thumb over his duty belt. "How did you know about the ax? That hasn't been made public."

"His sister told me." I watched his face. His nostrils flared. He wasn't liking this. "His widow confirmed it."

"So, what do you want?"

"Were you the investigating officer?" I knew his being a sergeant meant he didn't just roll out of cadet school.

"No. The investigation officer ain't with us anymore."

I hoped that didn't mean he was dead too. Now—this was the delicate part, only I'm not so delicate— "Well, Sir, I was wondering whether you would be so kind as to let me have a glance at your department file? I mean, what is the department's policy on that?"

"That would be a big fat no. The file is confidential, and if you knew anything you would know that. Anything else?"

Could he be any ruder? What happened to people in the South being gentile? "What about the autopsy report? Could I see that? They're public record." I wanted him to know I wasn't as stupid as he was saying I was.

"You want a copy of the autopsy report, you get it from the medical examiner."

"And where would he or she be?"

"You figure it out. Now, what else can I do for you?"

I politely declined to answer that question. He would not have liked my response. He went back inside the door to the right. I walked to the line of people formed to speak to the woman behind the window and waited my turn again.

When I arrived at the speaker thingy, I said, "Ma'am, I'm thinking because I saw sheriff cars outside that the Sheriff's Office is in this building somewhere, probably next to the jail?"

"Now you want to talk to someone in the Sheriff's Office?" Her eyebrows were raised, which gave me the impression she doubted it would do me any good.

"Yes, ma'am." I had opened my cell phone to the little notepad app, a yellow pad, a lined square with a yellow strip across the top. That's where I had the names of the two men Ben had given me. Maybe one or both of them knew someone who knew someone who would give me information on the investigation. Let's face it, you never know. "I'd like to speak to either Deputy Andy Crider or Deputy Rod Thibeaudx."

"Hang on a minute." She spit the gum she was chewing into a tissue and spoke muffled Greek again to someone on the other end of the intercom machine, or whatever they call them in these modern times. A few moments later, someone spoke muffled Greek back. Try as I may, I couldn't make out what either of them said. My guess is the design and the materials deliberately made it so outsiders couldn't hear what was said. She turned back to me. "Thibeaudx is on midnights. Crider is out on the mainland. He'll be back in at the end of his shift."

"Which is when, pray tell?" I rubbed my lips together and then did a full teeth grin.

Her right eyebrow rose. "I'm extremely limited on what information I can give you. You want to leave your name and number? I'll be sure each of them gets it. It'll be up to them whether or not they want to call you."

"Oh." Someone behind me cleared his or her throat long and loud. I didn't bother looking to see who it was.

"I really will be sure they get it." She smiled, and it went to her eyes. I had no choice but to believe her.

"Let me give you one of my cards for each of them." There was one of those drawers like you see at a gas station where they push it out and you drop something in it, and they pull it back in and take whatever you sent. She pushed it out. I put my cards and my trust in it. "Thank you, Officer." I gave her my best, real smile and stepped out of line.

Now what? The afternoon was coming to an end. Not a full bust, but not much accomplished either. I looked up the medical examiner's office on my cell phone. It was across the causeway in a smallish town called Texas City, not that far away. I walked back out into the still-glaring sun to my car and pointed it north. My phone had shown me the hospital where the ME was located, only twenty-two miles away.

The good thing about going into or out of Galveston was that there was a tall bridge over the bay from which I could see sparkling water and small islands, speed boats and barges, and brown pelicans escorting my car across. The bad thing about Texas City was the chemical smell that assaulted my nose as I grew close. I knew those chemical plants had to be somewhere, and they provided much-needed jobs, but that didn't mean I wanted to breathe the polluted air.

I found the hospital at what's named Mainland Medical Center. Funny, but though everyone knows Galveston is an island, the term "mainland" sounds odd to the ear of an outsider. Galveston County is made up of more than a dozen villages, towns, and cities and to think one of them is an island just seemed odd to me. I'm sure in Hawaii it's the same way when a native calls the other forty-nine states "the mainland."

After parking in the front and walking inside, I was told the ME's office was actually in a small building next to the hospital. Thanks, Cell Phone, you could have informed me of that, so I didn't have to get in and out of the car in the hot sun. But I did find it. An overcrowded space, cabinets and boxes filled the halls. I wended my way around until I found someone to speak with about obtaining an autopsy report. I was told yes, that's where they're kept. No, I can't just walk in

51

and get one. I would have to write them a letter requesting a copy. And mail the letter. In about one to two weeks, I should receive the copy if everything went well, or maybe sooner, depending, and then I could come back and pick it up. It's a good thing I'm a patient person and that I'd had a scrumptious lunch. I could afford to be polite even if I felt frustrated to bursting.

Well, I thought I'd try one last person, Chuck, the oldest son. I pointed my Mustang back toward the island as the sun moved toward the horizon.

Chuck lived two blocks away from his mother, closer to the beachfront in a one-story off-white brick ranch-style home. The lawn was so neat it could well have been trimmed with nail scissors. Showers of blooms cascaded from the huge plants. I hesitate to call them shrubs. They were just too large and luscious. I recognized the one with the yellow tubular flowers, Esperanza. And of course, bougainvillea in several shades of pink and red. A pleasant aroma, or should I say a mixture of aromas from the flowers, filled the air.

When I rang the doorbell, a young man, who I'm not kidding, could have been a male runway model, answered and stood in the doorway as though posing for a magazine cover, one hand on his hip. He was as tall as I and darkly tanned. He wore tight—when I say tight, you just have to take my word for it because I don't know how else to describe them—shorts, revealing, among other things, smooth-shaven legs. His feet were bare. A very short-sleeved turquoise muscle shirt fit him like his skin, revealing arms and abs like those seen in TV ads for workout machines. Long-on-top hair, which I think Candy said is called a taper because I asked once when her boyfriend showed up at the office and looked like he'd just stepped out of a barber chair. Do they still call them barbers? Anyway, his hair had to have been bleached, and then there was the diamond stud in his right earlobe, eyes that matched the color of the shirt and could have been colored contacts, perfectly formed lips—but I get ahead of myself.

"Are you Chuck?" Somehow, I didn't think so. Music played in the background. A saxophone solo. Nice.

Wide, perfect smile. "I'm Tim. Timmy to my friends."

"I'm Mavis Davis, a PI. I'm looking for Chuck." I had trouble keeping my eyes in their sockets, and my tongue in my mouth. Glad Ben wasn't with me. I figured the guy was gay, but still I couldn't help admiring his, well, beauty. "Isn't this his house?"

His snowy white smile revealed one dimpled cheek. "Yes, ma'am." His eyes took in the bandage on my face, but he didn't mention it.

"Is he home?"

"Oh, no, ma'am. Would you like to come in?"

Would I? I cleared my throat. "Thanks. It's a bit hot out here."

He led the way into a cool, small living room more than tastefully decorated, including a statue about the size of a table lamp, but it wasn't a table lamp. It was a male nude, in the flesh so to speak, but alabaster-white, not skin-colored. "Take a seat. Would you like something to drink, Mavis? Mavis Davis. That's so cute."

I sat on a white overstuffed chair-and-a-half and did my full teeth grin while not responding to that statement. "Just some water." Glancing around, the not-a-table-lamp wasn't the only art that signaled I was in the home of a gay couple.

"Oh, phooey on water. I'll bring you some lemonade. I'll be right back."

I tried not to look as he walked away. I closed my eyes and enjoyed the air conditioning for a few moments. The air had a spicy scent that reminded me of something I couldn't put my finger on, maybe someone or something from my childhood. Not my father. I hadn't really known my father.

When Tim returned, he handed me a glass of lemonade. "I hope that's okay. I make it with San Pellegrino water. It's all we have right now. I need to make a grocery run."

I swallowed a large mouthful. I didn't realize how thirsty I was until then. The lemonade was quite tart, but good.

He sat across from me on a white overstuffed sofa that matched the chair on which I sat. "Is that better? I thought you might be parched."

"Thank you. So—"

"Chuck's my partner. Or I'm his partner. Whichever way you prefer."

I nodded. Just as I thought. "Will Chuck be home soon? I'd really like to speak with him."

He did a one-shoulder shrug. "Supposed to be, but you know, Chuck is one of those guys who never met a stranger. He can get stuck talking for hours and hours. Well, not literally hours, but past time for him to be home. Is there anything I can help you with?"

This chatty guy could possibly reveal facts I might otherwise not be able to get. "Well, I don't know if it's appropriate or not…"

"You said you're a PI? That a private investigator, right?"

"Yep. And please don't make a comment about me being a female."

He tittered. "I wouldn't think of it. I bet it's exciting though, am I right?"

"It can be, though sometimes not so much." I took another sip.

"Can you tell me what you need to talk to Chuck about, or is it a secret?"

"No, secret. How long have you two been together?"

"A little over five years—seems like forever. In a good way, of course."

"Of course." I studied him. I was guessing Chuck could have been twenty-nine when his father was killed, if he'd been born within the year after the Lindens had married. I should have asked, but I hadn't. And if that were true, he'd be about thirty-four at the most now. And this young guy was probably younger than that, maybe still in his twenties, not that it mattered to me so long as he hadn't been underage when they'd gotten together. That didn't really matter either, except for the yuck factor, and Chuck would have been committing a crime.

But to get back to the murder... "So y'all were together when Chuck's father was killed?"

"Oh, yes, ma'am." He crossed his legs and leaned forward, his elbow on one knee. "You're looking into that? After all this time? Huh."

"I've been hired to help—since the police haven't been able to find the perpetrator."

"Oh, I see. Well, it was a terrible thing. Chuck was so very upset. It took a long time for him to get over it."

Which left me wondering whether he was truly over it. "I can imagine. Where did y'all live back then? Here in town?"

"Oh, yes. Chuck had just bought this house before we got together. Well, I should say closed on it. You know how that is. He and the mortgage company..."

I scooched around in the chair. If I'd been alone, I could easily have dozed off. Cool air blew down from the ceiling vent. The deep, soft chair wrapped me in its arms. And my body was drained from getting in and out of the heat all day. "Um, yes, I'm familiar with that scenario."

"Did you know Chuck was once a suspect? Is that why you're here?"

I perked right up. He'd certainly grabbed my attention. "He was once a suspect? But why?"

"Well, let me tell you." Tim dragged an ottoman close to me and sat down. He sighed and shook his head. "It was a terrible thing. We'd had a housewarming party here and invited all our friends and Chuck's parents and brother and sister, you know, the usual folks. I hadn't met Chuck's parents and was looking forward to meeting them."

Uh oh. I could guess what was coming next. I covered my mouth, so I wouldn't spew any little noises when he told me what I just knew he was going to tell me.

"Chuck can be so dense sometimes, I swear." Tim squared his shoulders. "I love the man, but really, sometimes..." He shook his head. His eyes filled. "He chose that occasion to come out to his parents. Can you believe that?"

I kept quiet and just nodded.

"You would have thought in these modern times that his parents would have figured it out long ago. I mean, I think his mother knew, really. She just never said anything. And, of course, the captain wasn't home that much, so you can understand why he maybe hadn't figured it out." His chin quivered.

Denial. Fathers frequently were the ones in denial.

"Chuck thought they would see all our friends and well, I'm sure you've noticed, our art." He raised his eyebrows.

"Yes, of course."

"Anyway, Chuck thought they'd figure things out, and he wouldn't have to actually say the words. Well, his father did figure it out." Tim rolled his eyes and shook his head. "He confronted Chuck in front of God and everybody. It was just horrible. He called Chuck names. And me, too, and our friends. We were so embarrassed, so humiliated." He looked like a hurt little boy.

"I can just imagine." A little pang where my heart was supposed to be made me reach out to him, like I was his mother or a counselor. I have no explanation for it. Tim took my hand. His grip, icy.

"So the captain, he said, and I'll never forget this, 'I'm glad you're not really my son. My blood. I'm glad you're only adopted.'"

"Oh my God," I said. I couldn't help it.

"Exactly." He squeezed my hand between both of his. Tears formed in his eyes. "Poor Chuck."

"What did Chuck do?" I set the glass down on a coaster and gave both my hands to Tim, letting him just about crush them in his anguish.

"Oh, Chuck was so—so shocked. So horrified. First, he looked at his mother, who hung her head, and then back at his father whose face was as red as your hair. See, Chuck didn't know he was adopted."

I didn't know what to say, so I didn't say anything. How could they not have told him he was adopted way before then and in a totally different way? How cruel his father was to have told him like that and in that manner. That was the first I'd heard that the captain wasn't such a great guy. But then, I'd really just gotten started on the investigation.

"Then Chuck stalked to the front door and slung it open and ordered his father to leave. They exchanged more words as his father escorted his mother out. Chuck slammed the door behind them and left the room."

All I could do was shake my head.

Tim breathed deeply and let it out, then released my hands and sat up. I sat back, too.

"And that's why the police suspected him?"

"Oh, yes. He was furious that his parents hadn't told him, and even more pissed that his father had treated him that way in front of all our friends. As far as I know, Chuck never had a conversation with his father after that. It's only been the last few years that he and his mother have gotten closer."

Well, that answered a lot of questions. And raised others.

Tim's cell played some pretty music. He answered it and walked into the kitchen where I couldn't hear. When he returned, he had some keys in his hand.

"I apologize, Mavis. I have to go pick up Chuck."

"Oh. Is he okay?" I stood.

"He still has some bad days. Today was so one of them. That call was from one of our friends. Chuck passed out in a bar downtown."

I patted his arm as we walked to the door. That maternal feeling really had a grip on me. "Okay, well, when he's sober, tomorrow or the next day, would you tell him I'd like to speak with him?"

"Sure." He opened the front door and gave me kind of a half-smile, half-grimace.

"Thanks for talking with me, Tim. You're a good man to stay with him, to take care of him."

He slipped his hands in his back pockets. "I can't help it. I love him."

I stepped outside and then turned back. "Oh, I forgot to ask. The police cleared him, didn't they?"

"Not really, Mavis." He edged the door shut, and I went to my car, my head spinning like a hurricane in the Gulf of Mexico. Not really?

As I pulled away from Tim and Chuck's house, I drove the two blocks to Roxanne's. I didn't drive in front of her house, just past the street. As I did so, the little yellow BMW drove away in the opposite direction. Making a quick one-eighty, I followed at a respectable distance. We drove north, then east, and finally north again into downtown Galveston. I hung back when he turned into a private parking lot. Easing into an alley from which I could view the lot, I waited for Platypus-face to come out of the fenced-in area. When he did, I chanced a huge parking ticket. I put on my emergency flashers and got out of my car to follow him. I didn't have to follow far. Not quite two blocks away, he entered a multi-storied brick building. I made note of the street name and number and ran back to my car and drove toward the West End. Time to find some take-out to take home—well, the place I was temporarily calling home.

Thirty minutes later, I carried some hot Chinese food up the stairs to the condo I was staying in and plopped down on the sofa. Fatigue would have grabbed me by the cojones, if I'd had any. Guess you could say it grabbed me by the ovaries. I put the bag of food on the coffee table and kicked off my shoes. My cell rang just as I got comfortable.

"Mavis, it's Isley. You have anything for me?"

I pulled my legs up under me and leaned my head back while we talked. I could use a nap, but WTH? I spent a few minutes giving Isley a rundown on everything I'd learned up to that point and promised we'd talk the next day.

No sooner did I sign off and stuff some moo goo gai pan into my mouth than I received another call. I tapped the icon and mumbled a hello.

"Yeah, this is Deputy Crider. You left a message for me?"

I perked up and swallowed partially chewed chicken and vegetables. "Hey, Deputy Crider. Thanks so much for calling. I was referred to you by my—by Lieutenant Ben Sorensen. You remember him?"

"Sure. Good old Ben. How's he doing?"

"Well, he told me you might be able help me with an investigation I'm doing."

"Uh—"

"Wait, hear me out. I'm not asking you to do anything that would get you into trouble. In fact, it has nothing to do with the SO. Ben said you used to work at the PD a few years back, and maybe you'd be able to assist me in some way. Maybe point me in the right direction? It's late today, but I was wondering whether we could meet maybe for lunch tomorrow? I'm buying."

He laughed. "All right. I just happen to have weekends off right now. There's a Tex-Mex restaurant I like on Broadway. Got a pen? I'll give you the address."

After we hung up, I felt energized. Someone with law enforcement connections was going to talk to me. I kicked back and finished my meal. Afterward, I jotted down notes on the day and questions I needed answered. The following day promised to be just as full. I stripped off my clothes, showered, and fell into bed feeling pleased with myself. There was nothing like a good murder.

Chapter 6

SLEPT IN AND DIDN'T EVEN FEEL ashamed of myself. I hadn't
been able to do that lately, sleep-in, not feel ashamed of myself.
After I crawled out of bed and fixed some coffee, I sat down and
wrote a letter to the ME, asking for a copy of the autopsy. I'd need an
envelope, which I would get later from the office supply store I'd seen
the day before. Then I jumped up with a brilliant idea. Grabbing my
cell, I phoned Lauren Smith and made a date with her for a bit later
that morning. Thirty minutes later, after breakfast and a shower and
still damp under the arms, I drove down the island. She was waiting for
me, inside in the air conditioning, of course.

"Hey, you up for this?" I asked when she let me inside. I didn't see
the dog anywhere and guessed she'd put in a room somewhere. She
was a lot shorter than I, way smaller than she'd looked when she'd been
leaning across the bannister a few days earlier. She wore a sleeveless
blue cotton dress with white fish block-printed on it and matching
blue flip flops. "We could go to jail."

She held up a key chain with one key on it. "I don't think so. They
still haven't changed the locks."

I clapped my hands. "You're kidding. Where'd you get that?"

"Roxanne and I exchanged keys when I moved here. Since we were the only ones here most of the time, we thought it might be a good idea to look out for each other."

"I thought y'all weren't really well acquainted." I hoped Lauren hadn't been trying to put something over on me.

Lauren led the way out the door. "I wasn't sure what all I should tell you. I mean, we're really only acquaintances, Roxanne and I. Just neighborly. She could be standoffish."

When we reached the bottom of the stairs to the former Linden house, I gave her a sideways look.

Her clipped white-blond hair glistened in the morning sun. She turned to me and grinned. "Really. Besides, I looked you up on the Internet and know you're legit."

I laughed. "Okay. That website my assistant maintains comes in handy sometimes."

Lauren jogged up the stairs and turned toward the beach. I followed her.

"I've been thinking about it since you left. There are two entrances to the house, not counting the elevator. This one that people familiar with the house use, even though it's in the back facing the beach and people have to walk under the house to get to it. And the front, more formal entrance that faces the road."

"Your point being?"

"Well, look toward the gulf. If someone had come up that way, they would have had to beach their boat way far down and walk all the way up here and cross over that walkover where the dunes are and be exposed. Of course, it was the middle of the night."

"You're good. Maybe you should be the private investigator."

She gave me a big smile, her eyes twinkling, as she inserted the key in the lock. "Let's go inside, and I'll show you what I mean when we get to the other door."

Inside, it didn't smell unlived-in yet. An aroma of flowery potpourri filled the air. We crossed the hardwood floor to the other side of the not-small house to the front door. She flipped a deadbolt, and we stepped outside onto the deck that faced the road. A light wind blew from the North and in the air, a chemical odor.

"See, if he or they came this way, they could pull the car right under the front door practically and run up these stairs and come in and do the deed and run out and jump into the car and get away really quick." She turned to me and waited for my response. "Or if he, she, or it didn't use the front door, they could walk under the house to the back door where we came in."

I leaned over the railing and looked down at the space where several cars could park. A car would have to pull in a bit down the way like I had and drive down to the Linden house, but that would take only a matter of moments. "A couple of things, though, Lauren. Wouldn't someone have heard the car drive up and then again when it left?"

She brushed at her windblown hair. "I see what you mean. They could have parked out on the road, but there's not much of a shoulder, and someone would notice a car parked out there—if they didn't flat out sideswipe it! Or they could park in front of someone else's house and jog down here and then run back."

"They couldn't assume that no one would hear them either way." I turned and leaned against the wooden railing and looked through the house to the other side. "No. I think they came from that way. It might have been more arduous getting in and getting out, but definitely quieter. They could have pulled a small boat up onto the sand way down the beach and worked their way back here. Because of the dunes, there's no way to see him, or her, really, until he crossed the walkover, but hell, he could have climbed over the dunes if he liked sand in his shoes." I turned back around. "And on this side, there are all the other houses that look out on the road. Even in the middle of the night, he still chanced some insomniac seeing or hearing him." I looked to her for confirmation that my idea was probably right. "Or them. Could have been more than one person."

"I'm assuming we aren't even considering that he may have come up in the elevator." Her eyes danced.

Chuckling, I said, "Uh…no." I was liking her more and more.

She put a hand on my arm and urged me back inside, locking the door behind us. "Don't want anyone to see us now."

I stood in the middle of the large downstairs, next to the stairwell. "I wonder how many square feet this floor is." The kitchen, a dining area, a humongous living area, the master bedroom, a guest bathroom with Mexican tile. All those rooms made up that floor.

Lauren shook her head. "Don't know. Ours is about two-thousand on the first floor though."

"This could be that. I want to take a look in the master." We trekked to the master bedroom. I would have liked to have seen it furnished. The room was half as large as the living area. Two long walk-in closets. A square-shaped bathroom with a toilet behind a private door, an oblong Jacuzzi bathtub, a separate shower, his and her sinks with cabinets under them, built-in medicine cabinets with mirrors and a row of cabinets and drawers separating them. More than impressive. I furnished the bedroom in my mind with a chest of drawers, a dresser, or more than one of each, which would have fit along the walls, as well as night tables and a king-sized bed. One window looked out upon the beach, and then I noticed a door leading out to the deck that ran wide across that side of the house. The perp could have used that door, if he or she could have gotten it open quietly. Another complication to think about. "Look at this, Lauren."

She pressed her lips together, her eyes wide. I was sure she was thinking along the same lines I was. "I wonder where the bed was positioned."

"For him or her or them to have knocked Roxanne out first, I would think they'd come to her side of the bed initially. So either the bed faced the entrance, and she slept on the right," I walked over to the far wall, spreading my hands to show where the bed would have been, "or the head of the bed was up against the wall to the right of the entrance, and she slept on the left." I returned to the doorway and indicated where the bed would have been and where she would have slept. "If he came through that deck door, he would have had to come around the bed to knock her out."

"So she could have slept on the left if the bed faced the door to the interior of the house."

"And he or she could have come in the deck door and knocked Roxanne out and then circled around to ax the captain."

"That sounds reasonable, if she was knocked out."

"Supposedly she was." We exchanged glances. I figured she was wondering about Roxanne being knocked out. I know I was.

"Did she have a concussion?" Lauren tapped her lips. "We had a case once where someone was knocked out, but I don't remember whether the person had a concussion or not."

"I don't know. Would you necessarily have one if you were knocked out? Or a scull fracture, maybe?" Isley hadn't mentioned that. Maybe Roxanne hadn't said.

"Something to check on. You can look it up on the Internet," she said. "If there had been carpeting, there would have been blood on the carpet on his side, don't you think?"

"Yep," I said. "I wish I could get my hands on the crime scene photos."

"Have you gone to the police department?"

"Yes. No dice. And the officer wasn't even nice about it."

"No surprise there. Do you know anyone who knows anyone?"

"I'm working on it. Let's go upstairs." Something creaked, like someone stepped on a weak board. Lauren heard it too because she looked at me with her eyes as big as half-dollars.

The stairs were wide and had a carpet runner from bottom to top. We climbed up and found a second living area with three bedrooms and two bathrooms. The bedrooms all opened onto the living room.

Two of the bedrooms were joined by a Jack and Jill bathroom. The other bedroom had its own bathroom, kind of like a second master but not nearly as large as the one downstairs. Of course, all the rooms had been emptied of furniture. We peeked into each room. There were windows facing the beach side in the second master and windows facing the street side in one of the other bedrooms. The middle one had a window that faced west, basically looking out on the house next door, not Lauren's.

"One of the sons, his wife, and their baby lived here with the parents at the time of the murder," I told Lauren. "That's what Roxanne said."

"That's what all the gossip says too."

Again, the floors were hardwood. Good stuff and well-maintained, shiny. "I really would like to know if there was carpet on the floors back then."

"Why, is that important?"

We walked back downstairs. "Supposedly no one heard anything. Carpet would help muffle screams, don't you think?"

Lauren nodded. "Probably, but if they were asleep…maybe they were deep sleepers?"

"Roxanne, if knocked out, wouldn't have heard screams. And if the kids were upstairs and asleep, it's possible they didn't hear anything. I'm just having a hard time believing that."

"What are you thinking? That they were somehow involved?" She led the way outside.

"I don't know. I just can't help thinking they couldn't have slept through someone chopping up the captain."

Lauren and I looked at each other at the same time. I got chills across my neck and shoulders. I didn't think I was coming down with a cold.

She locked the door. At the bottom of the stairs, I headed to my car, and she to her own stairs.

"If you have anything else I can help you with, Mavis, call me." She smiled really big over her shoulder and flashed her eyebrows, making herself look like a vaudeville villain. "I really want to help."

"I just might. Thanks a lot." Glancing at my watch, I saw I just had time to stop and buy an envelope and a stamp before I had to meet Deputy Crider.

As I drove away, I had the feeling someone besides Lauren was watching me. Could it have been the ghost of Captain Linden? I snorted. I don't believe in that stuff.

Do I?

Chapter 7

I FOUND THE MEXICAN FOOD RESTAURANT ON Broadway, not far from the post office. A little hole-in-the-wall, it was suspect, but if the cops ate there, it must be okay. The aroma of cilantro and beef met me at the door. I entered and glanced around to see if the deputy had arrived ahead of me. To the right of the front door, there were three booths full of what looked like office workers chattering away. Another three booths lined up to the left. Two full tables sat in the middle of the room under a donkey piñata strung from the ceiling. At the booth the farthest to the left, was one of the better-looking men I had ever seen in my life. He had jet black hair and a strong jaw, a Greek nose, high cheekbones, and full lips. When his radiant, clear, safari blue eyes met mine, I shivered. I know that sounds like something out of a romance novel, but I'll swear in court to what his eyes did to my body. I glanced at the other booths and tables. No one looked like they could be the deputy. When I glanced back, his eyes were still on me. I walked to the booth, my knees weak.

"You Deputy Crider?"

He stood, revealing not only that he was at least a good six inches taller than me, but that he had shoulders so broad, he could be wearing football pads. "Yes, ma'am," he said. There was that *ma'am* thing again, which this time I thought maybe was said not because I was old and needed respect, but because that's just the way cops talk, especially Galveston cops. I didn't hear that so much in Houston, even though I said it myself.

I held out my hand. "Mavis Davis." He took it in his large one but didn't engage in a bone-crushing shake. When he let go, I had lust in my heart. Not meaning to betray Ben, but damn, Andy Crider could make any woman wet her pants.

I scooted onto the bench seat opposite his. "Hope you weren't waiting long."

"Worth it now," he said, his smile not a leer but still suggestive.

I cleared my throat. The waitress came over. "Ready to order now?" She mostly kept her eyes on him. I tried not to.

"Iced tea and chile relleno," I said. No matter what Mexican food restaurant I ate in, I ordered chile relleno. I liked to see how different restaurants fixed them.

"Taco salad," he said, glancing at me. "Got to keep my girlish figure."

"Okay, now." I swallowed what I had been thinking and sat back and picked a chip out of the basket, dipping it in the red salsa.

He inclined his head toward the side of my face. "What happened there? If you don't mind that I ask."

"I resisted becoming intimate with a German Shepherd."

He snickered. "So, you're a friend of old Ben's?" He chomped down on a chip. "Mind if I salt them?"

"Go ahead. And yes, I'm an *old* friend of old Ben's." Was I being disloyal flirting like this? Probably, but it sure was fun and wouldn't go anywhere. I wouldn't let it. Damn.

"Haven't talked to him in a long time. He doing okay?"

"He said to say hi. Guess you know he made lieutenant a while back."

Crider nodded. "So, what help did he think I could be to you?"

Down to business pretty quickly. He probably had a date for an afternoon delight.

"I'm looking into an old murder case, and the PD isn't any help. Ben thought maybe you might know someone who wouldn't mind helping on the QT." I popped the chip in my mouth. Thin and crunchy, the way I like them.

"So. you're a PI?"

"I didn't tell you that?"

He grabbed a chip. "What's the case? I was with the PD for quite a few years."

"Yeah. That's what Ben said. The Captain Linden murder case, where—"

He held up his hand. "You don't need to tell me what it was about. I was on that case."

A little jolt ran down my arms. Lucky me. I hoped. "There was no way he or I knew that. He just thought you—"

"Might know someone who knew someone. I get it. No one is going to let you look at a file on an open case."

"I got that." I grinned. "But I bet you know practically everything that's in the file, don't you?"

"Pretty much." His forehead drew together as though he'd *put on his thinking cap*, as one of my teachers used to say.

"Or maybe you could somehow get me a copy or get someone to let me see the file just briefly?"

The waitress delivered our meals and my iced tea. For a minute or two, we busied ourselves with eating. For a hole in the wall mom-and-pop Mexican cafe, they sure knew how to stuff and roast a poblano pepper to my liking. I forced myself to take ladylike bites. When I looked up, his eyes were on me. "What?"

He shook his head. "Nothing. So you're with Ben?"

"Have been for years." I shrugged one shoulder, flattered that he would ask. "So, anyway, what do you think?"

"What do you want to know?"

"Just everything. Do you or did you have any suspects? Who were they? What the autopsy showed."

"That's everything, all right. So you know the basic facts, right?"

"Yes. I've met the widow. I've seen the house. I've read all the newspaper reports I could find, though there's not much in them."

"That's because we didn't tell them much. Not that we had a lot to tell."

"Even now?"

"As far as I know, no one is working the case. Five years is a long time."

"That's what my client suspected."

"Who's your client, the wife?"

I just stared at him and didn't answer.

He stared back. "Okay. What do you want to know?"

"Obviously you met the wife and probably the son who lived there at the time. What did you think of them?"

"Stuck to their stories consistently. The other son and daughter didn't live there, and I could find no motive at first."

"Meaning?"

"We looked at Chuck. Looked at him hard."

"Because of the fight he'd had with his father about his being gay?"

"Because of his anger at his father, and his mother, for not telling him he was adopted. When we talked to him, he was spewing cuss words right and left. Had nothing good to say about his father and not much about his mother either. Said he was glad his father was dead." He wiped his mouth and set his napkin back down. "The murder was clearly premeditated."

"But you couldn't pin it on him?"

He shook his head. "Not so far. He had an alibi. Home in bed with his partner."

"I met him—the partner. Seemed like a nice guy. Loves Chuck."

He raised his eyes to the ceiling. "I guess you could say that."

Was he a homophobe? If so, I didn't want to know. "He doesn't? He's been with him for a long time."

"It's just hard to believe someone could be so sincere. I mean, he's so damn *sweet. Humph.*"

"That he is. Some people really are that way, you know."

"Not in my line of business." He plopped a wad of ground beef and cheese into his mouth.

"And you ruled out the wife and the other son?" I cut a large piece of the pepper and scraped some rice onto it and put it into my mouth.

Andy chewed for a few moments and swallowed before answering. "Mavis, I haven't ruled out anybody."

I finished my mouthful. "Okay, well here's something I was wondering. Could Captain Linden have been involved in smuggling? I mean, those ships go to a lot of uh—exotic places. Couldn't he have made pick-ups of something?"

His eyebrows drew together. "Like?"

"What about people? Could he have brought back some people occasionally? Snuck them into the country? Put them in empty cabins and snuck them in? Could he have gotten cross-wise with some people for one thing or another?"

"Snuck in people past all the crew and immigration authorities and, let's see, who else? You have a vivid imagination."

"Well, someone was really pissed, to chop him up like that." I drank some tea.

"I'm eating."

"You're a cop. You gotta be used to it."

"Hey, I saw the body. Don't want to think about it when I'm eating."

I grimaced. "But they could have. I mean, he could have been involved with drugs too."

"Okay, look. We did check into that. I met with some of the crew."

"What'd they say?"

"One person mentioned the captain didn't get along with a lot of people, that he could be difficult, that he kept to himself except when he had to be charming, but there was one officer he didn't get along with. I checked the guy out, but he was on the ship when Linden died. He could have had someone else do it, but according to everyone I talked to, their rift wasn't bad enough to kill over."

"So in other words, you got nothing from the people on the ship."

"True, but I haven't ruled them out either."

"What about if he was smuggling drugs or something, and the crew wasn't involved? Did you find anything that pointed to that? Is that something you looked into?"

"Of course, and that's always a possibility, but we didn't find anything pointing to that."

"Hmmm. Maybe I could—"

"Hey," he said, putting his hand on my arm, "if you're thinking of pursuing that angle, don't. The cartels would make fish bait out of you."

I pulled my arm away, feeling a little burn at the suggestion I couldn't take care of myself.

"Let's finish eating and go to my apartment."

"Uh. I'm—" Speechless was what I was.

He leaned toward me. "I have a copy of the autopsy," he muttered in a whispery voice.

I about swallowed my tongue. I could barely breathe for a moment. The autopsy. Wow.

"We can talk privately there. Don't worry. I'm not going to hit on you." He flashed me a smile, showing one dimple.

"I wasn't worried." Too bad, though.

The waitress brought the check, and I took it. "I'm being paid for my expenses."

We finished lunch pretty much in silence, and I followed him to his place. I had to trust him. He was a cop, right?

He lived in a small townhouse on the East end of town, nothing fancy but clean and neat. Brown sofa and matching recliner. Tan curtains. Oak table and chairs. No rug on the dark oak laminate flooring. We didn't any more than get inside when I spotted a metal file cabinet against one wall. I wondered whether he had more than the autopsy in there, or if he was in the habit of sneaking files home on more than that one case.

"Why don't you sit at the table, and I'll get the report." He walked to the file cabinet and rifled through it while I put my purse down.

When he laid a couple of pages on the table in front of me, his musky, manly scent spoke to me, but I didn't answer. I didn't look at him for a moment. Couldn't. I glanced at the file cabinet, but he'd closed the drawer.

"Since you asked at the PD about the autopsy report, if anyone asks you about it, you got a copy from the ME."

"As a matter of fact, I went there, and they said I had to write a letter requesting a copy, so I wrote a letter and mailed it this morning."

"Perfect." He sat down next to me while I thumbed through it.

The injuries were as gruesome as I'd been told they were. The ME had made sketches, as well as attached colored photographs to the narrative which had been copied to regular paper. "Did y'all find the murder weapon?"

"Nope. Probably out in the Gulf of Mexico somewhere."

I studied the pictures of the corpse. Nothing unusual about it other than the injuries. There was a tattoo of a wolf on his right arm, but lots of people have tattoos, especially seamen. The body wasn't particularly dotted with moles. Years before, I'd had a boyfriend with many of them, and they were everywhere. This corpse only had a few. "There's no way to tell anything about the injuries other than they had been done with an ax? I don't understand how the ME could even determine that, but then I'm not much on science."

"Me neither, though I've learned a lot over the years. Did you know John Linden, that's the middle son, owned an ax?"

I reared back. "No way. His mother didn't tell me that. No one told me that."

"His sister told us that when we questioned her."

"It wasn't the murder weapon?"

He shook his head. "Nah. And I don't know what her motive was in telling us. I take it they don't get along."

"I don't know. I haven't met her yet. Where'd he get it? Why did he have one? That's kind of a weird thing to own." I looked at the injuries—which is a kind of sanitized description of what was depicted in the photographs. Pretty horrifying to see a body that looks a good deal like mincemeat. I couldn't imagine what the scene must have been that night at the Linden residence.

"He'd been in Toronto once when they were having a throwing contest, so he attended and liked what he saw and bought an ax. It's really more of a hatchet. We executed a warrant to search the whole house, you know how that is, and found it in a suitcase under his bed. There wasn't anything on it. Looked pretty unused."

"Strange coincidence, though. I haven't met him yet, either. His mother says she doesn't know where he lives."

"I can believe that. Last I heard, his wife divorced him, and he drifts from place to place."

"So you're keeping up with this case?"

He looked at me. "I guess I can trust you. See that file cabinet? The whole top drawer is the Linden case."

"That you're not supposed to have."

"That I don't have. You never saw it."

"I haven't seen it yet, either."

"Want to?"

"You don't have anything better to do on a Saturday afternoon?"

"I know you're going to think I'm crazy, but there are some cases that just don't go away. This is one of the few I made copies of and brought with me. I can't leave this alone. Every once in a while, I pull it out and go over it, looking for something I missed."

"And you don't mind sharing?"

"Hell, if you can help, why not?"

The table had nothing on it except the autopsy report, so when he started bringing Pendaflex files out of the cabinet, there was room for him to set them on the table in some kind of order known only to himself. We spent the rest of the afternoon reviewing them. Each witness had their own thin—or not so thin—manila folder. Each Pendaflex file had a label listing what folders it contained. Pretty organized. There was a file marked "Witnesses" that contained those folders. We started there. One thing I learned immediately was that although Roxanne Linden hadn't had a skull fracture from being knocked out, she did have a sizable goose egg. She had spent the night in the hospital, so they could observe her.

And after reviewing all those pages for all those hours, I didn't learn much else. Although Andy had interviewed and re-interviewed people, they always gave him the same story. The evidence never changed. He knew the weapon. He knew where and when the crime took place. What was needed was a motive, and so far, Chuck was the only person who had one.

Chapter 8

"HEY, TIM." I STOOD IN FRONT of Tim and Chuck's door again, figuring early evening on a Saturday night might be a good time to catch Chuck. "He around?"

Tim was dressed in white Bermuda shorts and an orange Polo shirt. A real Polo, not a knock off. It had the emblem and everything. He held the door wide, sweeping his hand in front of him like a *maître d'* inviting in a guest. "He's asleep."

I glanced at my watch. Time for dinner, not sleeping, unless you were a shift worker.

He closed the door, and we went into the living room again. "I'll go wake him. It's been, like, a whole day."

"Since yesterday? Wow."

He nodded. "This is what he does. He didn't use to, but after his father's death, he got worse and worse until now, after a bender, he can sleep for what seems like days, except for getting up to use the toilet."

"Doesn't he work?" I sat down on the sofa and got out my cell phone. I could check my emails while Chuck was getting up.

"Supposed to, but he hasn't sold any houses lately." He frowned. "We're going broke." He left, heading for the bedroom.

What did Tim do to make money? I scanned my emails. Mostly junk. Margaret checked in, even though it was a Saturday. Since we lived alone, we had this agreement to email at least once a day to make sure the other was still alive. I emailed her back that I was okay. Candy had sent me a message asking the same thing, as did Ben. I had three keepers, but I didn't mind, most of the time.

Tim returned. "He'll be here in a couple of minutes. He's freshening up in the bathroom.

Peeing and washing his face and hands, I hoped. "Thank you."

"Want something to drink?"

I shook my head, and he sat down on the ottoman. We looked at each other for a few minutes. I put my cell phone away. Chuck came and stood in the doorway. He was about six feet tall, thin as a knife blade, had a full head of dishwater blond hair, and a three-day-old growth on his face. His body was wrapped in a thick, navy blue, terrycloth bathrobe. I walked to him and held out my hand. He looked at it and finally shook it, his hand about as limp as a dead squid. His body odor smelled almost as bad as a dead squid.

He almost stumbled on his way to the easy chair, falling into it. "What do you want?"

So that was how it was going to be. "I'm—"

"I know who you are and what you do for a living. I want to know what you want from me."

Tim said, "How about I get you a cup of coffee, hon?" He wasn't speaking to me.

Chuck looked at him and raised an eyebrow. "Put a little something in it besides caffeine."

Tim shook his head and left the room with a glance at me first, his mouth screwed up in a frown.

"Your aunt hired me to see if I could help find out who uh…who killed your father."

He sat with a hand draped down each arm of the chair. His bathrobe had fallen open, but luckily it was large enough that he wasn't exposing his family jewels. "You mean my biological aunt or my adopted aunt?"

I wasn't going to play with him. "I only know of one aunt. Isley Gibson."

"Don't know her."

"Be that as it may, she was your father's only sibling. She's afflicted with COPD, now lung cancer, and is terminal. She wants to find out who killed your father." I straightened up, trying to appear indignant. "If it's of any interest to you, she has a small estate that she'd like to leave to his family."

His demeanor didn't change. "Including me?"

"As far as I know."

"Still don't know her. Never met her. Never even heard of her when my father and I were still speaking."

"Yeah, and I'm wondering about that. Why do you think your father failed to tell y'all you had an aunt?"

"Beats me. He never told us much about anything having to do with his life."

"Didn't you find that strange when you were growing up? I mean, that you never met your grandparents or anyone on his side of the family?"

"The captain was a disturbed individual. I didn't really know that when I was a kid, just thought all fathers were like him, closed mouthed and strange." He adjusted his robe. The tension passed out of his shoulders, allowing them to come down from around his ears.

"See, that's the first I've heard of that. Your mother didn't tell me anything like that, but then again, I didn't ask her. I was focused on the events surrounding his death. So your father was kind of weird?"

Tim returned with a yellow mug of coffee the size of a cereal bowl.

The aroma dominated the air, and it was way better than Chuck's aroma. Kind of warmed the tense air that was already draining from the room. He handed the coffee to Chuck. "Mind if I sit in or want me out of the way?"

"It's fine," Chuck said and sipped from the steaming cup.

Tim sat opposite me on the ottoman again, his legs and arms crossed. "I was just telling her how strange the captain was." He looked at me. "Timmy is the only person I've ever really talked to about the captain. I tried with my mother, but she never would listen."

"So what else did he do that was weird?"

"You know he was a control freak, right?"

"I did not. Again, that's the first I've heard of it, but you're only the second person I've spoken with who knew your father. So tell me what you mean by that." Some peoples' definition of "control freak" was different from others. It had become a popular label of late.

He swallowed big from his cup. "Okay, look, he was gone all the time—well—most of the time, but when he was here, I could hardly breathe. He insisted on driving my mother everywhere, like to the grocery store and even to her church meetings." He set his coffee cup on the side table. "Same with us kids. If we had a ball game or practice, he would drive us, wait 'til it was over, and then bring us home. He decided where we would go, what we would eat, even what we'd wear. When we came downstairs, we had to line up and let him inspect our clothes before we went anywhere."

"Does seem a little odd, considering he was gone a lot of the time. What did he think y'all did while he wasn't there?"

"Man, I don't know. Maybe he put us out of his mind. Maybe he treated the crew like he did us, though that would have been impossible. He couldn't have gotten away with that." He shook his head. "I have no idea what went through that madman's mind at any time. But one thing I'll never forget, when he got home, if we didn't show him straight As on our report cards, *whack*." He made like he was swinging at someone. "We'd get the belt."

My stomach lurched. I'd never been hit by my mother or my father, but then again, my father had always been in absentia. Still, I could only imagine how awful it would be to be hit by a parent.

"Like how? I mean, some pops or what?" The coaches when I'd been at school would give pops to the boys if a parent had signed a permission slip. They'd use a wooden paddle. I'd once walked past the open gym door and seen it. Gave me the creeps.

"I don't know what he did with my sister, but with me and my brother, he took us into our room and made us drop our pants and really gave it to us."

Tim had pain in his eyes and looked away. Feeling squeamish, I sank back on the sofa.

Chuck took a really deep breath and released it. "All these years later, and I can still hardly stand to think about it." He picked up his cup again and gulped the coffee down, holding the cup out to Tim. "Need more."

Tim took the cup and left the room.

"Did your father beat your mother? Did you ever see him hit her?"

He shook his head. "I remember when I was little, really little, I would hear her scream sometimes at night. Not when I was older, though. Sometimes I wonder if I'm just imagining things." He stared hard at me and gritted his teeth. "God, I hated that man."

"Enough to kill him?" I stared back, hoping my expression was as deadpan as I was trying to make it.

Chuck didn't answer. When Tim returned, he gave Chuck the cup again and perched on the arm of Chuck's chair, his hand resting on Chuck's shoulder.

"Tell me about the night of your father's murder. Had you seen your parents that day—for their anniversary?"

Tim said, "They were really on the outs, Mavis. Remember I told you what had happened at the party?" He glanced at Chuck. "Yesterday when she was here, I told her about the party. Don't get mad."

Chuck said, "I'm not mad. I vaguely remember you mentioning it on the way home."

"The captain didn't want to see us together," Tim said. "He wouldn't let me in their house."

If I'd known the man, I might have killed him myself. "So did y'all or didn't y'all see them on their anniversary?"

Chuck said, "Timmy thought if we—I—went out there and took them a gift, maybe it would help mend fences. Not that I cared whether I ever saw the man again or not, but my mother, well, I do love my mother in spite of everything."

"So we bought his mother a dozen white roses and his father a carving knife with pearl inlay in the handle. You know, pearl for a thirty-year anniversary."

"Yeah, the captain thought the white roses were like to symbolize a happy marriage, but really, we bought them as sympathy flowers." He and Tim laughed together from deep down inside themselves. I had to smile. Their laughter was contagious, though I wondered whether the deep laughter was to mask horror and sobs at the whole situation.

When they stopped, Chuck wiped tears from his eyes. Or maybe he didn't wash his face well enough, and it was really sleep. I don't know, but the whole situation was really awkward. I just sat there and waited to hear the end of that story.

Tim said, "I drove Chuck out there and waited in the car. Chuck went inside, wished them well, gave them the gifts, and we left. The whole thing didn't last ten minutes."

"Five minutes," Chuck said. "I hugged my mother and gave her the roses. After they were through exclaiming over the flowers, I tried to shake hands with my father, but he wouldn't take my hand, so I just pushed the box at him and said, 'Happy Anniversary,' and left." He glanced at Tim. "That's the last time I ever saw him."

"Was your brother there when you were there?"

"I don't know. John and Vonnie stayed upstairs with the baby as much as they could when my father was in town. I didn't stop to see whether or not they were home."

Chuck was shifting around in his chair, tying and retying his robe. I had a lot more questions but thought that first meeting was a good start. A couple more things, and I was out of there. "How do you get along with your brother? Are y'all close?"

"We were in high school, especially after we'd get a licking from the captain. Not anymore, though."

"When was the last time you saw him?"

He shook his head.

Tim said, "John shows up on our door step every now and then."

"You know they're divorced, he and Vonnie?" Chuck said.

I nodded. "And so, where does he live? He doesn't live with your mother."

"I can give you the number of a friend of his that might know, but I have no idea. I don't think he has a job." Chuck took a long swallow of coffee.

"What about Vonnie and the baby? Where are they?"

"The baby's not really a baby anymore. But I don't know where they are either. John would know. He probably doesn't pay child support, but he and Vonnie have always kept in touch. Give me your email address, and I'll email you John's friend's name and number." He got up, indicating, as far as I was concerned, that my time there had come to a close.

I handed him a card. "Thanks for talking to me. I hope you don't mind if I give you a call sometime if I have more questions, or if I stop by."

"I don't care. You can if you want." He gnashed his teeth. "I want you to know one thing, though, Mavis. I didn't kill my father. I wanted to sometimes, but I didn't. And I don't care what my aunt wants. I don't even care if you find out who did it."

Isley and I might be the only ones who did.

Chapter 9

FIRST THING SUNDAY MORNING, I CALLED Hanna Beth Linden, thinking I'd catch her before church or before she went to her shop. In Texas, most places open around lunch time on Sundays, so working people can go to church. I don't know what they do out there in Seattle.

As soon as I stated who I was and what the call was about, Hanna Beth hung up. I had hoped it was just a dropped call or disconnect until it happened the second time.

The third time I texted her. "Hang up, and I'll just come see you in person." I didn't especially want to go to Washington State, but if I had to, I'm sure Isley would have paid my way. Once my phone said the text had been delivered, I called again.

The phone stayed silent for about five-seconds before she said, "What do you want from me?"

"Thank you for answering. Your aunt hired me to find out who— uh—who killed your father."

"You've got the wrong person. I don't have an aunt, at least not on my father's side."

That was getting old. How could someone not know anything about a parent's family? "Believe it or not, you have an Aunt Isley Gibson. I haven't quite figured out why none of y'all ever heard of her. That's something we may never know since your father is deceased."

"So where's this aunt been all my life?" Sounded like Hanna Beth was warming up to me.

"The military and California. Says she lost contact with your father several decades ago."

"Weird." She cleared her throat. "He told me my grandparents were dead, and he didn't have any brothers or sisters or even cousins. That's what he said ever since we were little."

"Yes, ma'am. That's what I've been told."

She laughed, a tinkling little laugh in my ear. I said, "So anyway, Isley has COPD and lung cancer and wants to find out information about your father. She'll have a small estate and will probably leave it to y'all."

"I don't want her money. I don't want anything to do with any of the family. I'm assuming you spoke to my mother. She should have told you that."

"Is there something no one is telling me about why you feel that way?" Personal question, but WTH?

Several seconds went by again. "I don't even know if you're who you say you are. Why would I tell you anything?"

"You could look me up on the Internet. You could call your mother or Chuck."

"I just said I didn't want anything to do with them. Why in the hell would I call them?"

Maybe she wasn't warming up to me. "Look, Hanna Beth—"

"Out here I go by Wendy."

Now that was weird. A complete change of first name, not associated in any way that I knew of. I'd heard of people dropping their first name and going by the second or dropping a nickname when they grew up and going by a more formal first name, but to change her name completely meant, to me at least, she had reinvented herself. "Okay, Wendy. I'm not trying to upset you. I'm just trying to solve the murder of your dad."

"All right, listen here. I've hardly been back to Galveston since way before someone killed my father—which was probably justified, by the way. All I know is he was killed with an ax. You sound like a nice woman, so I don't want to be rude, but I have nothing to tell you. Nothing. If you want information, you need to talk to John Wayne. He's the one who owns an ax. Goodbye." The phone went silent.

Clearly, she wanted to shock me, and I would have been shocked if I hadn't already known about the ax. I thought about calling her back but decided it would be fruitless. I spent a few minutes thinking about our short conversation. Wendy was hostile to the whole family. She wasn't going to feign any interest or take responsibility for anything related to them. By telling me about the ax, she either wanted to shock me or point suspicion away from herself or toward her brother or all three. I wondered whether Andy Crider had considered her a suspect, whether he'd found any motive for her to have done the deed. I couldn't remember any discourse between us about her.

After dressing and eating some breakfast, I hopped into my car and drove east on the seawall to the address Roxanne had given me for John Wayne Linden's friend. The time still being before noon, the beaches weren't as crowded as they would be later in the day. People were, however, already out and about, running, walking, skating, and bicycling on the seawall. Some were sunbathing on the sand. One man waved a metal detector around as he paced to the water's edge. People were fishing from the long pier that extended into the Gulf and from the granite rock groins. I thought about what it would be like to live in Galveston. Would I be one of those people who took advantage of the geography or one who took it for granted, never leaving my house except when I had to?

Al Smyrna, John Wayne's friend, lived on the first floor in an old house that had been divided into four apartments. The neighborhood was either in the middle of a renaissance or slowly deteriorating. Every house appeared to be in transition, peeling paint, unattended yards, cracked sidewalks, and overgrown trees.

I parked as close to the address as I could, there being vehicles sitting in front of most houses, and walked the rest of the way. No one was on the street. The area was quiet. I wondered whether people were late sleepers for various reasons—like shift workers or up dealing drugs all night.

The doorbell was missing half its plastic cover, so when I didn't hear it echo inside the building, I banged on the wooden screen door. Hadn't seen one of those in a long while. About a minute later, a tall, thin man who appeared to be in his thirties pulled the door open. He had dark hair, sleepy brown eyes, and a couple of days' growth on his face. He wore a T-shirt that said *Galveston*, faded jeans, and was barefoot. "Yeah?"

"Al Smyrna?" There was another door open behind him. One I assumed led into his apartment. The aroma of fried bacon had followed him out the apartment door to the front door. My stomach growled, in spite of the fact that I'd had a bowl of cold cereal, one of the few supplies I'd stocked in the condo kitchen. I pressed my hand on my abdomen and hoped he didn't hear its request that he share his meal.

He smiled one of those knowing smiles that said he had heard the growl, but he was too polite to mention it. "Yeah, I'm Al."

I looked up at him. I couldn't very well stick my hand out to shake because the screen was between us. "My name is Mavis Davis." At that, he repeated the smile. "I'm a private investigator hired by John Wayne Linden's aunt to assist the police in trying to figure out who killed

Captain Linden. I understand you're a friend of John Wayne's. Does he go by John Wayne or just by John?"

"You want to come in?" He pushed on the screen, opening it wide enough for me to slip past him and into the house.

Out of the corner of my eye, I caught him glancing at my bandage. My guts fluttered. No one knew where I was. Roxanne knew she'd given me the man's contact information, but I hadn't shared it with anyone, even Andy Crider. I made a quick decision to go ahead and trust the man, even though I was wincing inside. I'd spent several years going into people's homes when I worked for the county and made home visits. That had always turned out all right for the most part. Al and I made eye contact as I stopped in the foyer.

"Don't worry, Miss Davis. I won't hurt you."

My face grew warm. I didn't want him to know I felt uneasy, but it was too late for that. "I trust you, Mr. Smyrna." I followed him to the back of the apartment, to the kitchen, where a plate of bacon and scrambled eggs and an English muffin graced a green Formica table in the center of a kitchen furnished with outdated appliances and furniture.

He dropped into a chair. "Mind if I finish eating? I hate cold bacon and eggs."

"I'm so sorry to interrupt." I stood with my keys in my hand until he asked me to sit. I took a chair adjacent to him. "So, uh, John Wayne is a close friend, would you say?"

He scooped some egg into his mouth and nodded. "Since kindergarten." He swallowed from a cup. "Yeetch. Cold coffee. Want some?" He pushed back his chair and went to a coffee maker on the counter.

"No thanks. Had mine."

He sat back down. "Yeah, John and I went all the way through school together and graduated from Ball High. That's our high school." He continued to eat.

"And remain friends to this day." It was more of a statement than a question.

"Yep. He crashes on my couch sometimes. He doesn't have any place to live."

"What can you tell me about him?" I held my hands and my keys in my lap.

"He's had a bad time ever since he got divorced."

"So he's not working? Does he own a car?"

"Rides a bicycle. He found the bike laying out by some trash cans on trash pickup day and fixed it up."

I mentally corrected his English but, of course, didn't say anything aloud. He sounded, for the most part, fairly well spoken. "That's his only mode of transportation?"

"Unless he can get one of his friends to take him somewhere."

"Like you? Does he have many other friends?"

He slurped some coffee. "Three or four who help him out. Been doing it for years."

"Seems like it would get old after a while." I studied his profile. A scar crossed the side of his chin. His nose wasn't quite in alignment. But his attitude was okay, not threatening.

He pushed back from his plate. "Hell, we've been covering for each other since we were kids. Been through a lot together, and so have some of the others."

"What do you know about the family?"

"*Humph.* Father was a jerk. Mother wasn't great about protecting the kids. Or herself either, for that matter."

"It's weird to me that John Wayne and his wife would move in with his parents when by all accounts Captain Linden was—"

"An asshole. You can say it." The corner of his mouth twitched. "They moved in when he was gone. Didn't think they'd be there when the captain returned, but John Wayne couldn't find another job."

"You know his siblings?"

"His siblings?" His eyebrows rose. "You mean his brother and sister?"

The corner of *my* mouth twitched. "Yes. Chuck and Hanna Beth."

"It's hard not to know people in Galveston when you grow up together and all go to the same high school. This town is not really a small town, but it feels like it."

"How did the other kids get along with their father?" I was looking for confirmation of what I already knew.

"I think Chuck got picked on the most. What do you call it?"

"Scapegoating?"

"I don't know why. Well, I do know why now, but I didn't know why then."

"And why was it?"

"He was adopted. No one knew until they were grown up." He got up and walked to a smaller table pushed up against the wall. He shook a cigarette out of a pack and lit it. "I mean the kids didn't know."

I waved my hand in front of my face. I'd quit and was past the stage where the smoke smelled good. He didn't say anything, just sat back down.

"What about Hanna Beth? Did the father pick on her, too?"

"He picked on all of them, just Chuck the most."

"So that's why Hanna Beth wants nothing to do with them? But if he didn't treat her as bad as the boys, why doesn't she want to have anything to do with any of the family?"

He rocked back in his chair. "Okay, I'm just going to tell you. I know I shouldn't, but I don't see how it matters now. John Wayne can get mad if he wants." He took a long drag on his cigarette.

"Did the father sexually abuse her?"

"No, it wasn't that. At least, I don't think so. Hanna Beth got PG in high school, and her father made her give away the baby."

A little twinge of pity tweaked my belly. That answered one question. "But she doesn't really speak to her mother."

"Their mother didn't stand up for her."

That didn't explain why she didn't want anything to do with her brothers. "And the boys?"

"I'm not sure what's up with that."

I stared at him for a moment. I didn't know why he'd revealed so much, but I was grateful. I figured if he knew why she wanted nothing to do with her brothers, he'd tell me. "Do you know of any reason someone would want to kill Captain Linden?"

He chuckled. "Anyone who'd had any dealings with the asshole."

"No, seriously."

"Seriously." He laughed again.

"Do you think John Wayne or Chuck could have done it?"

"Maybe Chuck, but not John Wayne. I mean, he and Vonnie were right upstairs, and Vonnie would have known, and I don't think he would've wanted her involved in it." He shook his head. "Not John Wayne," he said again. "Besides, he didn't have as much anger as Chuck. I mean, John Wayne stayed out of it most of the time."

"What does that mean?"

"He was stoned, man. Any chance he could, he'd get high."

"I didn't know that."

"Yeah, that's why Vonnie ended up leaving him. She loved him, but he kept getting worse and worse. He couldn't keep a job. He'd lose them when he'd fail the drug test, or he'd get high and not go in. His father used to yell at him that he wished they'd never wasted their money on sending him to college."

"He told you this?"

He looked at me for a moment. "We used to get high together."

"Used to?" This guy was a wealth of information. Too bad he didn't know who killed the captain.

"I'm on probation now. And John Wayne doesn't have any money that I know of."

I flinched. Since I was alone with him up in his apartment, I hoped he wasn't on probation for anything violent. And then I wondered about that last bit. Did he mean John Wayne might be dealing?

"For selling dope," Al said, as if he could read my mind.

"You or John Wayne?"

"Me. I'm on probation for selling dope. I don't know about him."

I sighed hard. I was running out of questions. "Okay, so let me ask you this. Did the father do drugs?"

He slammed his hand on the table, making things rattle. "Shit, no! He'd never use, and he thought he could beat it out of John Wayne."

Would Isley want to know that? I thought if Captain Linden had been my brother, I wouldn't have wanted to know all that. "Could he have been involved in something like selling drugs? Like getting them on his trips and bringing them back and selling them?"

His face screwed up. He shook his head.

"What about other stuff, smuggling art or something else or people, maybe? Immigrants?"

"Man, if so, I don't know anything about it and don't want to know either. That's serious shit."

"Who might know? Do you know anyone who might know?"

He got up and lit another cigarette. The first one was still smoldering in the ashtray.

The air had changed in the kitchen, and it wasn't because of the cigarette smoke. His back was to me. He straightened his shoulders as if he'd reached a mental resolution. When he turned around, he said, "You seem like a nice lady. Are you sure you want to go there?"

When he put it like that, I wasn't so sure. Isley had hired me. I'd taken her money. So far, I hadn't regretted it. I looked into Al's face. His expression had turned more than serious, grim, warning-like, his lips pressed together. He rubbed a finger across his lips.

"I think I do," I said. "Clearly you're thinking I shouldn't?"

"I'll give you the name and last address I have of someone who might be able to give you information, but it didn't come from me."

My thumping heart beat out a warning, but I had a job to do. "Okay, thanks."

He tore a piece off a paper drugstore bag, the kind a prescription comes in, and wrote on it. Handing it to me, he said, "It's an old house, like this one, a quadplex. Near the old jail—the courthouse." His eyes rested on my face a moment. "If you go there, be careful. Most of the neighborhood is probably safe, but…"

Chapter 10

LEFT AL'S, BUT INSTEAD OF GOING to the address he'd given me, I drove to another of John Wayne's friends' houses, the friend Chuck had told me about. That house was situated in what appeared to be a better part of town, at least the homes all looked like single-family.

Rapping on the door several times and getting no response, I considered the possibility the friend was at church. After all, Sunday is the day many people participate in that custom. No one was around in that quiet neighborhood. No one mowing lawns. No one walking a dog. So, either church or late sleepers. I scribbled a message asking the man to please call and stuck my card in the door. I wasn't standing out in the heat and humidity any longer than I had to.

What to do? What to do? I could go *to the scary house* Al had told me about. I could go downtown and sit outside the coffee shop I'd spied, in hopes of seeing Platypus-face. I wanted to know who he was and what he was to Roxanne. I could go to Houston and get the charger for my laptop and retrieve my gun from the gun safe while no one, specifically Ben, was around to discourage me. I chose the latter.

If, after that, I were to go to *the scary house*, I would be armed and dangerous, though hopefully not to myself.

Also, if I drove back to Houston on a Sunday afternoon, chances were Ben might be off work. He might want some company. He might want more than that. I knew I did, a whole lot more.

I put my Mustang in D and headed toward the causeway and home. First stop, my office, which wasn't far from my house. The drive took an hour, more or less. I felt sneaky when I arrived at the office. Of course, no one but me ever worked on a Sunday unless we had a dire emergency, and when did that ever happen? I parked in the rear and entered through the back door.

First thing I did was go to the safe and get my .38 and a box of rounds. I felt like I needed to look over my shoulder, that Ben might be watching me. He was so against my carrying a gun. Seemed like everyone else in Texas carried, why not me? Ben didn't care about everyone else, he said. And even though I'd told him I'd feel safer with it, he still worried about me.

Anyway, I didn't stomp, but I didn't tiptoe, back to my car where I locked the gun and the rounds in the glovebox. Didn't want Ben to catch me. What a coward I could be sometimes. Not really, but I did like to avoid a fight. Fighting interfered with our love life.

Returning inside, I checked the mail on my desk. There was only a bit of it. After all, I'd only been gone a day, though having been in a different city made it feel like a lot longer. I saw nothing that needed my immediate attention. Then I looked in on the rest of the office to make sure everything was as it should be. What could happen in a day wasn't something I wanted to contemplate. I knew Margaret and Candy could get into trouble in significantly less time than a day, but to my surprise, everything looked fine. Candy's hairbrush sat next to the faucet in the bathroom sink. Margaret's sweater still hung on the back of her secretarial chair in case the air conditioning made the office too cold.

I sat down at Margaret's desk and wrote her a note, telling her I might want her to come down and spend a day or two in Galveston with me. If someone needed watching or something else came up that required assistance, I could use her help. Margaret could be helpful outside of the office if I could get her to focus. The condo in Galveston had two queen-sized beds, so there wouldn't be any extra expense.

As I finished the note, my cell rang. Caller ID showed Isley. "I was just getting ready to phone you, Isley," I said. "What's up?"

She cleared her throat. "I haven't heard from you lately."

Which wasn't true, but whatever. I started to tell her I was in Houston at my office, but she didn't need to know that. "I guess I didn't call you last night. Well, anyway, I touched base with your niece yesterday, Wendy."

"I thought her name was Hannah Beth." Isley coughed a long, jagged-sounding hack.

I waited until all was quiet on the other end. "Yes, well, she changed it to Wendy." How much information did Isley really need to know about Wendy? How much personal information that wasn't related to the case? Isley was my client. Wendy wasn't. Still and all, I saw no need to tell her everything I learned from Wendy, the private part, the part about being forced to give away her baby, at least not at that moment.

"A name change. That's strange. Don't you think?"

"It happens, especially if someone has had an unhappy childhood."

"Which you suspect Hanna Beth had?"

I blew out a long breath, not quite a sigh. "I think your brother was abusive to all of the children. And probably to Roxanne, as well."

"Humph. Don't like to hear that."

"Well, I can tell you there was no love lost between the children I've spoken to and their father. I haven't met the middle child yet, the one who was there the night of the murder." Feeling kind of antsy, I picked up a pen and started drawing stars on Margaret's desk pad.

Isley issued a ragged breath. "That makes me sad."

I started to make a wisecrack about which thing made her sad but thought better of it. "I've pretty much ruled out Wendy as a suspect in the murder. She lives in Seattle. She's been estranged from her family for a long, long time. There's no indication she's been back here or had interaction with any of them. I wish the same was true for Chuck, the older son."

"Do the police suspect him, too?"

"He hasn't been excluded as the perpetrator. Briefly, I can tell you that he was mistreated horribly by your brother, treated differently from the others because, it turns out, he was adopted." I caught myself bearing down hard on the pen I'd been doodling with and threw it down. "He was humiliated, shamed, in front of friends and his partner. Chuck could easily have planned the murder. He knows the island well. He could have pulled it off."

Isley coughed again. I wondered whether she could be getting worse so quickly or whether she was just having a bad day. When she stopped coughing, she said, "I wanted my brother to be a great guy. I wanted him to be the hero I remembered from when I was a child."

I didn't know what to say, so I didn't say anything.

"Our father didn't abuse us. Neither did our mother. I have a hard time believing the brother I remember could have matured into a mean man." Her voice became softer. "He was the type of boy who would move a turtle out of the street, so no one would run over it."

"Nevertheless…from the two children's telling of it, he was a control freak. Had always been one since they were little. What strikes me as odd was how he'd be gone so much of the time but expect them to kowtow to him when he was home. But—"

"That's not so odd. I've heard of men—in the service or otherwise employed where they were often away from home—not liking it when they returned home to find the family had been doing well without them, living independently, and really didn't need them."

She took a moment to clear her throat. "A lot of military families have difficulty adjusting."

What she said didn't surprise me. A lot of people, not just men, have a lot of issues stemming from what life had dealt them. "So, anyway, I've been looking for John Wayne, the middle child. Since the murder, his life has fallen apart. He's divorced. His wife took the child and left. He's unemployed and homeless."

"You know, Mavis, this isn't what I was hoping to hear. I mean, Roxanne wasn't forthcoming, but I was really hoping the family was intact."

"I'm just telling you what I've found."

"I know." She let loose with a horrific cough again. When she stopped, she said, "I think I'm going to ring off. I'm really not feeling well today and have heard enough anyway."

"Wish I could give you better information."

"Call me tomorrow?"

"Sure. Take care of yourself, Isley." My chest felt weighty. The situation was sad all the way around. I wished I could have helped her in some way.

After she clicked off, I headed to my private office in the back of the house to get my computer charger. At the same time I reached my doorway, the back door, which I stupidly had forgotten to lock, opened. Adrenaline spiked my gut until Ben loomed, then my heart broke into a smile.

"Just happened to be driving by my office and stopped when you saw my car?" I was unable to hide my pleasure at seeing him. I gave him a big smile.

He reached me in one quick stride, a grin on his face. "Just checking on the premises as I always do if I'm in the neighborhood." He pulled me into his arms. "How are you, baby?"

I put my head back where I could see his face. "Hungry and ready for an afternoon delight." Whereupon he laid a juicy kiss on me. When we came up for air, I said, "Just let me get the charger for my computer, and we're out of here." I wanted to get on with our personal business, get into our separate cars, drive to wherever we were going for lunch, and I hoped he wouldn't question my driving all the way to Houston just for my charger.

Chapter 11

ARMED WITH MY CHARGER, NOT TO mention my gun, when I arrived back in Galveston the following morning, I stopped by the condo to retrieve my laptop. I had several ideas I wanted to follow up. None of them included going to the scary house just yet. I headed downtown to Mod Coffee House, which I'd spied when I'd followed Platypus-face, or rather half-followed him. Mod is a two-room coffee house. One holds the actual store part—coffee bar, cakes and cookies, and refrigerated goods. The other room is like a large family room full of well-worn, cozy furniture and small tables—the preferred room of students and small groups. I went inside and purchased an iced coffee something or other before parking myself at one of the black wrought-iron tables outside under an awning. If my rear end hurt too much after a while, I could go inside and fall into one of the comfortable-looking easy chairs. For now, I was on the job. In the meantime, from where I was, I could look right across the street at the building into which Platypus-face had gone. After making myself at home, I logged onto the Internet via the free wi-fi and searched for what was in Platypus-face's building.

Condos. Should have figured that. Everything had been and was turning into condominiums, almost in front of our faces. I finished my drink, packed up my computer, and marched across the street.

The place was pretty fancy, higher dollar than I could afford, but I never let that intimidate me before. Well, not too much. Orange and vanilla scented the air. Indoor-outdoor carpet covered the bit of floor in the lobby. A staircase ran parallel to the elevator.

"May I help you?" a more-than-decently-dressed woman behind a counter asked. In fact, her outfit looked like something I couldn't afford either. But what the heck?

"Good morning. This is a nice place," I said. "What is it? What's in this building?"

She looked me up and down. "Very *expensive* condominiums. Are you lost?"

She looked at me as though I must be, there being no other reason for me to have entered. "I'm in the market for a condo. I just wasn't sure I was in the correct place." I gave her a smile that was mouth only. She probably didn't notice the narrowed-eyed look, reserved for people like her and suspects. In the detective rule book, number 58 or maybe 85, I'm not sure, I think it says to only use that look when being treated like something stuck on the bottom of someone's shoe.

"Uh-huh." She eyed me up and down.

"How many floors in this building? Four? Five?"

"If you already know, why are you asking?"

"I don't already know, ma'am. I just looked at the building from the outside and made an educated guess."

"Educated?"

She was starting to get my ire up, but no way would I let on. "So how many square feet? I imagine they vary, right? Maybe twenty-five hundred and up?"

She tilted her head and raised one eyebrow.

"Did I guess right again?" In a minute, she'd probably figure out that I looked at their informative website. 'Til then, I'd enjoy myself. "Okay, so with traffic being the way it is in downtown Galveston, I imagine one of the attractions of this place is its private parking, am I right?"

"Evidently you already know the answer to that too."

"Yeah, I know parking is part of the deal, but where exactly do the owners park? And where do guests park? And how many spaces do the owners get? Does it depend on how many occupants are in each condo? And by the way, are there any owners in residence right now whom I could talk with about what it's like living here and whether or not I should consider buying a unit?" I was thinking *whom* was the correct word, hoping it was. Wanted to impress her with my vocabulary. Now why was that?

She crossed her arms, flashing a diamond bracelet on one wrist. What did they pay receptionists nowadays? "A block and a bit away in a private lot. Wherever they can find a space on the street. One space comes with the condo. No. Owners may purchase another if there any available. And no." Her smile stretched almost from cheek bone to cheek bone.

She was good. I'll give her that. It took more than a moment or two for me to remember just exactly what I'd asked her and to mentally match up her answers, but I figured out that she wasn't going to let me talk to any of the owners whether or not any of them were on the premises. I could think of a few choice names for her.

"Can you tell me the names of any of the owners, so I can get a reference from them?"

"I most certainly cannot."

She'd been sitting at the desk behind the counter during our exchange, and when the outside door to my right opened, and a youngish, blondish woman entered carrying a Mod Coffee House cup that smelled like spicy Chai tea and a bag I could only guess held a sandwich or croissant, the diamond-braceleted woman stood and came from behind the counter.

The youngish woman exchanged places with her and said, "Thanks so much, Mrs. Worthington. You're so sweet to give me a break." She set her refreshments down on the desk and took her seat.

Mrs. Worthington strolled to the elevator and inserted a key into a lock. "You're very welcome, Abigail. Call me again if you need anything." The elevator door opened. She stepped inside and gave me a smirk as the doors closed in front of her.

Aww, she got me good. I had to appreciate the woman, even though a part of me wanted to call her names and not just in my head. I turned to Abigail. "So was that one of the owners?"

"Yes, ma'am. Another girl is supposed to come in for my breaks, but she's sick today, so Mrs. Worthington said she would spell me for a few minutes. She believes in taking care of employees. Oh." She put her hand to her mouth, her eyes wide. "Who are you?"

I swear I did not laugh. "Oh, just a prospective buyer. Mrs. Worthington told me all I needed to know, however."

"Did she give you a brochure?" The girl pulled a brochure from the top desk drawer and brought it to me. "The website is listed inside."

"Thank you so much, Abigail. You're a doll."

I left and crossed the street where I again went inside and bought a drink. I always felt funny using up space at someone's business if I didn't spend money there. I know, I know. I had just bought a coffee a bit earlier, but I can't help the way I feel. While I waited for them to mix an iced coffee something different from the first one I'd imbibed, I glanced around. The place was really pretty cool, glassed in with small tables between the counter and the doors, an upstairs about the size of a small bedroom, and that connecting room with sofas, easy chairs, and stools up against a bar facing out floor-to-ceiling glass. People appeared to love it, judging by their constant ingress and egress. I glanced across the street toward the condos, and a thin man who looked like he was in his seventies came across and into the Mod. *Hmmm.*

When my drink was ready, I meandered around the coffee shop, looking at the mixes one could dump in her drink and at the breads and scones and sandwiches and vegetable juices, and when the seventies-man walked into the connecting room, I followed him. I sat down on a chair next to where he sat. I sipped my drink and opened my laptop. I pretended to be working—actually made a few notes and casually started up a conversation with seventies-man.

"This is a pretty cool place." I sipped my coffee, looking at him over the top of my straw.

"Um? Uh, yes, it is." He had a shock of white hair and clear hazel eyes. "You've never been here before?"

I shook my head. "First time. You live around here?"

He nodded toward the condo building. "Across the street. Moved there when I retired last year. I like having no yard to mow."

"And you can see the cruise ships from here."

"Sometimes I walk down there and wave at people when the ships cast off. Name's Ian."

His lifestyle sounded sweet. I held out my hand. "Mavis. I'm from Houston. I was kind of thinking I might like to move down here. The pace is much slower, isn't it?"

"Much, though sometimes cars race down Postoffice Street like they're in the big city. That's the street out front."

"Yes. So what's it like in your condos? Are there a lot of units, or are the condos real big so only a few people live there?"

His brows drew together. "Sort of middle-sized, I guess. The top ones are the largest. I don't live in one of those, but I've been inside. Pretty damn nice. But mine is too, just not as plush."

"I guess everyone who lives there is retired? I'm not retired. I'd have to find a job somewhere south of Houston. I wouldn't want to drive all the way back up there every day."

He held his cup with both bony, liver-spotted hands. "Nope. There's one or two who work out of town. A drug salesman. He's gone a lot of the time, mostly here on the weekends. His wife is an artist, pretty good too. They could be retired. I don't know why he still works." He looked from his left to his right. "She's a trust baby."

I raised my eyebrows at him to convey that I understood. "Would I have seen any of her work? I mean, is she any good?"

"If you come to the Artwalks here about every six weeks, you can see some in one of the galleries. There's another artist too. He likes to go out on the roof and paint with the wind blowing in his hair." He chuckled. "His words. He's pretty good too, if you like pictures of the wharves and pelicans and seagulls."

"I do."

"And a woman who was the first female mayor of some town up by Dallas. Don't know where she got the money..." He glanced sideways at me, like I was supposed to know what he was implying. I pretended I did. We spent a few more minutes. He described as many of the tenants as he could remember without my urging, I might add, until he drained his cup.

I wondered whether any of the men he'd told me about was Platypus-face. "Let me buy you another cup of coffee, Ian," I said, swooping down and taking hold of his cup and saucer. "Be right back."

Chapter 12

WHEN I RETURNED WITH A STEAMING cup of coffee for him and some carrot cake for me, which I knew I shouldn't eat but was going to anyway, Ian was conversing with a woman who looked to be his age, sixties to seventies. Who could tell these days. Not me. His wife? I handed him his drink and sat back where I'd been.

"Mavis, this is Etta. She's one of the artists I told you about who lives in my building."

We shook hands. She smelled like linseed oil. "Mavis Davis."

She didn't laugh at my name or even look like she wanted to laugh. I appreciated that. "Henrietta Downs, but I go by Etta. Nice to meet you." She wore a long, gray braid down her back, and bangs covered her forehead. She had iridescent eyes that appeared to change shades of blue when they turned from focusing on Ian to me. Her clothes were what I'd call artsy-fartsy, sandals, long colorful skirt, and tank top.

I had sat forward and shoveled a bite of cake into my mouth. Both people watched me. I swallowed. "Nice to meet you too." I held out the plate and fork. "Want a bite?" It seemed to be the only polite thing to do, even though after taking that first bite, I realized my heart would break if they said yes. "Or you can go get your own fork. I won't dishonor it with a cliché like it's to die for, even though *it's to die for*."

"We know," Ian said. "But, no thanks."

Etta shook her head and thumbed the waistband of the long skirt she wore. "You're looking at the evidence."

She wasn't at all fat. I ate another bite and set the plate on the coffee table, next to my computer.

"Ian tells me you're interested in a condo in the downtown area." She had perched on the arm of an overstuffed and just-about-worn-out easy chair.

"Casually. I've only just begun checking them out."

"What others have you looked at besides the building we live in?"

I was going to do my best not to lie, at least not to tell any whoppers. "None, yet. I drove around downtown Galveston the other day and liked what I saw, so I came back to get some information."

She nodded and slid down into the chair proper. Ian sipped his coffee, his eyes bouncing from one of us to the other. Etta said, "Do you have a price range you're thinking of?"

"Not yet. Just trying to see what's available and whether it would even be feasible. I was telling Ian that I'd have to get a job down here. I wouldn't want to commute to Houston." I eyed the carrot cake, my mouth watering for more, and sipped my coffee. Lukewarm. Yuck.

She glanced at Ian. "I've been thinking I might want to put mine on the market."

"Really?" Ian said. "I didn't know that."

"Just starting to give it some thought." She clutched Ian's forearm. "Please don't mention it to Jeffrey," she said, her eyes changing shades of blue again.

What was that about? Was there something between Etta and Ian? Was Jeffrey her husband?

"Jeffrey's my husband," she said. "I haven't mentioned it to him. I'm just thinking about it. I might want to leave Galveston."

"Now that'd be a shame," Ian said. "You have so many friends here."

So maybe there wasn't anything between them. They were just friends. But when she said she was thinking of moving, she used the singular. Hmm.

"Anyway," Etta said, "if you're interested, you could come over and see it. My husband's out of town right now."

"You'd let a complete stranger into your apartment? That's not a very safe thing to do."

She cocked her head. I wasn't trying to give away what I did for a living and hoped I didn't put my foot in it.

She said, "I just thought—well, you look okay to me." She chuckled. "If you were seriously interested, we could both save money by not going through realtors."

"True," I said, feeling a bit guilty. I wouldn't let guilt stop me from seeing the inside of one of those condos, though.

Ian's brows drew together. "This is sudden, isn't it?"

"My parents could use some help. They're ancient, you know, and live outside of Kerrville."

"Aren't they in a nursing home?" Ian shifted in his chair, giving her his full attention.

She glanced at me and back to him. "Yes, but if I lived near them, I could visit frequently and be sure they're getting proper care."

Ian's lips pressed together in a frown. Did he know more and not want to bring it up with me around? I took another bite of carrot cake and watched the two of them. There was some nonverbal communication going on.

"So anyway, Mavis," Etta said, "when you finish your cake, I'll take you over, and you can see my place."

"I wouldn't mind seeing some of your artwork, as well." I pushed the plate with the remaining cake to the center of the coffee table and dabbed at my mouth with the napkin. "I'm ready when you are."

She brushed Ian's bare forearm with the tips of her fingers and stood. "Um, we bus our dishes around here. You don't have to, but most people do."

"Okay." I picked up my plate and cup. "Ian, you coming with us?"

"No, but I'm ready to go. I'll walk y'all across the street."

After we handed over our dirty dishes, Etta led the way out the westside door and onto the sidewalk. Though a number of people sat in the shade provided by the awning and vines and ficus trees, when the blast of humid hot air hit me, I was glad I'd originally chosen to go inside.

As we walked past, Etta pointed at the window of the gallery next to Mod. "I have a few pieces here, but I can show you some in my apartment."

"She's really very good," Ian said. "You'll be impressed when you see them."

I smiled my response. I felt a bit awkward for several reasons, one of which was my subterfuge, but another was accompanying two complete strangers into a building where I knew no one. They could be serial killers. I didn't think they were, but they could be. Unfortunately, I'd left my gun in my glovebox, but times like these I appreciated the invention of cell phones, so I'd be able to call for help.

We crossed the street and entered the building, which, of course, was air conditioned. Even with the short walk from Mod Coffee House, I'd broken a sweat. Abigail was still at the desk. I flashed my eyes at her and said, "Hey, Abigail." If she was surprised to see me in the company of two of the owners, she hid it well. With a twinge of apprehension in my stomach, I followed them inside the elevator. Ian got off on the second floor.

"I'm on three," Etta said when the doors closed. "There're four floors. The top floor is divided into two huge apartments, really ostentatious, and they have the best view."

"So Ian told me. But you probably have a pretty good view too."

The elevator opened, and we got out. "Yes, and every owner has the right to go onto the roof. Every once in a blue moon, I go up there to paint. There's another artist who does, as well. Jeffrey and I sometimes go up there to lay out—sunbathe."

I followed behind her. "I thought sunbathing was passé." The hallway floor was covered in sand-colored, deep pile indoor-outdoor carpet.

"Have to get my fifteen minutes of sun, right?" She grinned over her shoulder. Her weathered face looked like it didn't need more sun, but it wasn't my place to suggest sun screen.

A painting hung on each wall on the way to her apartment. "I thought it was fifteen minutes of fame."

"Maybe it's ten minutes of sun." She shrugged and put her key in the lock. "By the way, those aren't mine." With a nod, she indicated the paintings hanging in the hall.

I was relieved. I don't know much about art, but I thought they weren't all that good. Apparently, some decorator's idea of art. Probably hung before anyone knew artists would be residing in the building.

The air was even more refrigerated when we entered Etta's apartment. I stopped in the doorway, momentarily stunned. The fact that she was rich practically slapped me in the face. If I hadn't known she was a trust baby, I would have thought she was a famous artist, or had married money, or was into successfully dealing drugs, or had some other possibly illicit source of income. Her apartment was decorated like a five-star hotel. Not that I'd been in many five-star hotels. Okay, maybe none.

I hid my astonishment as best I could. I mean, I knew people who lived in downtown condos had to be well-to-do, but this was over the top, at least for me. Ben and I, and most other people with whom I'm well-acquainted, are definitely working-class. The only other wealthy people I've known were other clients, like some in River Oaks in Houston, and some lawyers and doctors I'd been a client/patient of or with whom I'd had other business.

Exquisite, very thick, Oriental rugs that had to have been hand-knotted were layered over hardwood floors in the entryway and the living room. A crystal chandelier hung in the entry way, another in the living room. A comfortable-looking furniture grouping that looked like Fendi Casa was centered in the room together with lamps in coordinated colors and tables that looked like mahogany or could have been something more exotic. The only thing I knew was her furnishings looked similar in quality with what I'd seen in River Oaks in Houston when I'd investigated a case there. Boy, did I feel out of place. And who was I fooling? Did this woman really think someone like me could afford to live in a place like that?

I set my purse and laptop on an entryway table and followed her as she gave me the grand tour. She led me to the bathroom and bedroom. She pulled back the drapes and let me see the view. "Fantastic," I said. If I'd been there on Sunday instead of Monday, I would have seen a great view of a docked cruise ship. She took me into the kitchen.

"Want some coffee or tea?"

Her kitchen would be a cook's idea of heaven. As for me, I thought it was pretty and modern and knew, even if I could afford to live there, it wouldn't get much use. "No, thanks. I'm saturated. I'm still learning to like it. Was a tea sip, but coffee is so in—" I was babbling, so I shut up and slid my hands into my pants' pockets.

She put her hand on my arm and gave it a slight squeeze and said, "I'll show you my studio on the far side, away from the bedrooms, and would you like to go up on the roof?"

"Sure, while I'm here." I swallowed. My mouth was dry. I guess I could have used a drink of water but was eager to see the rest of her place.

Across the room, she took hold of the doorknob. "I want to warn you. Some people have trouble with the smell in here." She opened the door wide.

Luckily, even though I have a strong sense of smell, I don't have allergies. I can tough out almost any odor for a few minutes. If I'd had congestion, it would have cleared out fast from the ammonia smell, or maybe it was another solvent which overwhelmed the oil paint smell. How could she stand it? I blinked my watering eyes.

The room had a hardback wooden chair up against the wall right next to the entrance. An easel stood in the center on a drop cloth. In fact, the floor was covered with drop cloths splattered with varying amounts and colors of paint. A second easel stood across the room in a corner. A large painting in vivid blues and greens and browns and grays and more rested against the wood frame. I'm guessing the familiar-looking street scene was of a street I'd traveled somewhere in Galveston.

The piece on the easel in the middle of the room was only partly finished, though a sketch of what the final picture would be had been made on the canvas. A jazz combo of light and dark-skinned people stood playing mostly brass instruments, like trumpet and trombone, on the bed of a truck in a Mardi Gras parade.

Pretty much the rest of the room was what I'd expect an artist's studio to look like, with paintings stacked up against the walls, a few hung, paints clustered on shelves, brushes standing in jars, and even an artist's pocketed smock hanging from a hook.

I glanced at her to see if she had any response to the air in the room, but she only looked back at me with what I interpreted to be a proud smile. "Sorry if the odor's too strong. I think I became used to the smell years ago."

"You're really talented." Which made me wish I had some talent other than snooping into other people's business.

"Thanks." She urged me back out the door. "Let's go up to the roof, and you can get a deep breath of fresh, salty air."

She didn't have to tell me twice. I went back into the living room. "I really appreciate the grand tour."

"You're quite welcome. I've enjoyed living here." We walked back to the entrance. "I'm giving you my card with my phone number, so you can call if you're interested. Think it's a possibility?"

I pocketed her card, which had a picture on it that I thought looked like her painting style. "I don't know, Etta. I'm guessing it might be out of my price range." I really wasn't guessing. I already knew it was—even if I'd wanted the condo, I could never leave Houston. Ben was there, and my office, and the girls, and I'd built up my business. Certainly I wasn't, and probably never would be, in the position to buy a second home. Why was I thinking about all that anyway? How unrealistic to even contemplate it. I was on a case, that was all. Speaking of which, I'd spent way more time in downtown Galveston than I'd intended to.

"You don't have to decide now." She locked the door behind us and directed me to a door at the end of the hall. "We can get to the roof from there."

"Okay, but then I really have to go. I've got some things I need to do today."

She nodded. "No problem. I was thinking we could have lunch, but I guess not." Her wistful tone surprised me.

"Maybe another day?" I gave her what I thought of as my cheery-comforting-smile and followed her down the hall.

"All right." She took hold of another key on her keyring and unlocked the door. "I usually make a sandwich or a salad. I just thought since I'm already on a break from working, I might as well have lunch out."

I wanted to accommodate her, but I'd planned to go to the scary house. I'd worked up my courage and wanted to get it over with. "I can call you or text you and maybe later in the week?"

"Or you can catch me most mornings at Mod. I get up early and get some work done and go over there most days for coffee before hitting it again."

"Yeah. Okay." I followed her up the stairs.

"We have two flights to get past the fourth floor. I hope you don't mind the stairs. I find them easier than the elevator—unless I'm carrying something. The elevator can be slow if someone else is using it."

"No, that's fine."

She stopped and turned to me. "I sound pathetic, don't I?"

I backed up a step. "What do you mean?"

"Like I don't have anyone to have a meal with. I'm sorry. I don't mean to sound needy."

"I didn't think that." Maybe a little, but I wasn't going to tell her. I liked her. I wouldn't mind having lunch with her at all. I really would get back in touch with her since it looked like I'd be around Galveston at least for a few more days.

She continued climbing the stairs. "My husband is a salesman. Pharmaceuticals. He's gone a lot of the time."

"Uh-huh—like every day?" She was lonely is what she was saying.

"Most days. He doesn't have to work, but he likes having his own money."

I didn't respond.

She stopped again and turned halfway toward me. "He has some investments from an inheritance, but it's not enough for him. I'm not sure anything would ever be enough for him."

I nodded like I knew what she was getting at.

She started up again. "See, I'm the one with the real money. The condo is mine, not ours. I bought it with my trust fund."

"I see, so if you sell it..."

"If I sell it and leave, he's not going with me. Once he runs through his investments, he'll be out on the street. I don't know because I don't ask, but I imagine he has only enough money to buy a small place of his own. We keep most of our money separate."

"Oh, well with a job, he can get a mortgage."

"That's right. *Humph.* I'm sure he could if he wanted to, though he recently spent a lot of money on a car he'd had his eye on for a long time. A stupid little car that a much younger man should be driving."

Finally, I could see the landing at the top of the second flight of stairs. I thought I was in pretty good shape, but my breath wasn't coming as easily as it should have.

"Almost there. I don't know why I'm telling you all this, Mavis. Just explaining why I don't have plans for lunch, I guess. Not that I'd want to eat with Jeffrey all the time." She reached the door at the top and pushed it open.

I didn't know what to say to that last statement. She didn't sound like she'd like to eat with him *most* of the time. I couldn't see her face, so I didn't know for sure whether the sarcastic tone was intentional. I suspected it was.

The salty air was welcome when we walked out onto the gravel-covered roof. I could see why any artist would like to paint from there, although no one was doing so right then. In the cloudless sky, no sane person would want to be up there at that time of day. It was too damn hot. A ship was plowing past now, headed out to sea. We walked to the edge and looked out on the buildings across the street, the gallery and Mod and the ones opposite. We could see all the way down Postoffice Street. Then we walked to the south side and could see all the way up Twenty-second Street to the Gulf of Mexico, a sparkling strip of blue in the distance.

We were about to go over to the west side when a little yellow car raced around the corner and began parallel parking.

"That's Jeffrey," Etta said. "I wonder what he's doing home on a Monday? He should be miles from here."

It was Platypus-face. A sphincter muscle of mine flexed. He

glanced at the building and down the street and back at the building and headed toward Mod.

"Well, I need to go." If I hurried, I might just be able to get my purse and laptop and get the heck out of Etta's condo before he arrived. At least I hoped so. I didn't want to meet him head on. At least, not yet.

Etta looked my face over. "Okay, well keep in touch."

I strode toward the stairs. I hadn't really thought about Etta being the one married to Platypus-face, so I wasn't prepared for how to handle any situation that might occur. I wasn't sure where he fit in with the captain's case, if he did. I just needed to get going, so I wouldn't have to meet him, and it wouldn't be an issue.

Etta closed the door behind us and shuffled down the stairs behind me. I was not going slow. I reached their floor and pushed the door open and hurried down the hall, Etta close behind.

She unlocked the door and let me inside. "I hope I didn't do anything to offend you."

Shaking my head, I grabbed my belongings and backed out into the hall. "I'll be in touch in a few days. Thanks for showing me around."

Her bewildered expression pulled at my heart strings, but I had no time to explain and wouldn't know how anyway. "Goodbye." Jogging to the elevator, I said a little prayer that I wouldn't meet her husband as I made my exit. I punched and punched and punched the button until the elevator showed up. A tiny shiver ran down the back of both arms when I got on. The elevator creaked downward. The door sprang open on the first floor. I rushed out and waved at Abigail. I saw no one on the street. Quick as I could, I pushed through and walked in the opposite direction from the coffee house, never looking behind me, even when the back of my head prickled.

Chapter 13

AFTER I REACHED MY CAR AND took several deep breaths and a swallow of water, and my hands quit shaking, I gave some thought to what my plans were for that afternoon. I'd been lucky in the past few minutes but didn't want to press it.

Instead of going directly to the scary house alone, I phoned Lauren. "You up for driving to the East End? I want to use you for back up."

"Oh, heck yeah. When are you talking about?"

"Not exactly backup but as a lookout."

"What are you going to do, rob a bank?"

I liked her. I really did. She had my sense of humor. "No bank robbery today, but I'm going to see a person of interest. How do you like that FBI-type term?"

"And you want me to go with you or what?"

"Kind of like call the police if I never come out."

"What? Are you sure you should do this? Sounds like you'll be putting yourself in danger."

"It's all part of the job." I'd never admit the thought made my stomach churn, but if she thought about it, she'd realize that's why I wanted her to be there. "Can you come or not?"

"Like now? Right this minute?"

"If you could get downtown in forty-five minutes, that'd be great. I'm going to grab a sandwich, and I'll meet you there."

"Where exactly? And what do you want me to do?"

I gave her the address and explained what I wanted and went for lunch. Exactly forty-five minutes after our phone call, I parked around the corner from the scary house. Moments later, Lauren pulled in behind me.

She jumped out of her car and ran to my window. "Hey, girl." She wore white jeans, a starched. white blouse with a white and black print kerchief tied around her neck, and white running shoes. I wondered what she thought we were going to do.

I climbed out and gave her a quick hug. "His house is the one in the middle of the block. So if you could, find a spot where you can watch the door. I'll wait until you park, and then I'll venture over there."

"You didn't say who this is. Whose house is it?"

I met her eyes and tried to mask the forbidding feeling that must be showing on my face. "A very bad dude I'm hoping to get information from, if not on."

"And all you want me to do is watch the house?"

"Yes, just in case. In fact," I pulled a card from my pocket, "I've written the name and phone number of a law enforcement officer I know on the back of a card, but don't call him unless it's been an hour or so. Okay?"

"Oh, Mavis, you're kidding—right?"

"I have to talk to this guy." A laugh erupted out of me, sounding like a hiccup. Was I nervous or what? "Or if someone comes out carrying a bag—a large bag—or a trunk. Or even a large suitcase."

"Okay, now this isn't funny." We'd both been leaning against the front of my car. She jumped in front of me as if to block my way. "Why are you doing this, really?"

"If you don't want to help—"

"It's not that." She grabbed my upper arm. "You're scaring me. Who is this man, and why do you have to see him?"

"Okay, my client's nephew's friend gave me his name as someone who might have been involved in my client's—uh—well, you know, Captain Linden's death. Or at least know something helpful. The police have never interviewed him or even the friend who gave me the info. Hopefully, this guy will just give me some information."

"You've got me really confused." Her eyebrows squished together. "What you're saying is this person—this man—might know something about the murder, so you have to see him instead of the police?"

"Uh huh. Exactly."

"I still don't like the idea, but if you're determined to do it, at least I'm here to watch your back." She headed to her car. "Or watch for your back as you come out the door." She snorted. "Give me five minutes."

I gave her my best grin. I was lucky to have met her. I could have called Margaret or Candy to come down to the island and help me out, but since Lauren volunteered, I didn't have to. With Margaret and Candy, I always stood the risk of them blabbing to Ben about what I was doing if he gave them anything resembling the third degree. Ben didn't know about my new friend. I would have to take her out to a big expensive seafood dinner when the case was over.

I waited five minutes and walked to the house. The neighborhood was an old one with cracked sidewalks and large oak trees. From all appearances, most of the houses had been refurbished, brought up to date, but there was the occasional hold out. The house in question was one of those.

Lauren had found a spot where she could observe the front door. I hoped she wouldn't be there long enough to warrant a ticket for parking too long.

The house was up high off the ground with lattice-work covering an area surrounding the part from the first floor to the ground. I couldn't tell if there was anything under the house, behind the lattice. Just darkness. There were about a dozen worn, wooden stairs and a balustrade on each side with light blue peeling paint. Sweating, and not just from the humid Galveston heat, I gripped the railing and looked up toward the glassed-in front door. A thin white curtain hung behind the glass. When I arrived at the top, I could see a foyer and a staircase leading to another floor.

The door opened easily. There were two metal mailboxes embedded in the wall on each side. An apartment door stood next to the mailboxes. Three of the four mailboxes had slots with white paper inserted inside, with names written on the paper. None of the names were the one I had been given. The nameless one was up those stairs. I wasn't breathing hard from the first set of stairs, but when I looked up at the next set, or should I say two sets—a number of stairs, a landing, and then another set of stairs until the top landing—I drew a deep breath to settle myself down and started my trek to the top.

Patting my back pocket, I confirmed that I had my cell. I didn't care what anyone said, a cell phone was better than nothing. If I had a chance to call for help, at least I'd have that. I'd left my purse under the seat in my locked car along with my gun in the glovebox, which I had conflicting feelings about. I didn't think a person like me would look very friendly if I was packing. I could just picture someone of the criminal element frisking me, or at least giving me the once over, and seeing it. That would be the end of a quote-unquote *friendly* interview.

Reaching the apartment landing, I paused for a couple of breaths and stilled my hands before knocking. The door was plain and black and worn around the doorknob. The wooden floor could use sanding and a coat of whatever that clear stuff is that is used to cover wood floors. The peephole stared me right in the eye, so I knocked sort of medium hard, kind of hoping no one would be home. Blotting my damp forehead, I stepped to one side and waited.

The door squeaked open. No one was there. I half-expected someone would be hiding behind the door and holding a gun on me through the crack. The distinct aroma of weed mingled with tomato sauce wafted through the doorway.

In response to the clearing of a throat, I looked down into black-as-onyx eyes. No, it wasn't a dog—for which I was grateful. In front of me, or rather in front of about the first four or five feet of me, stood a little person. She wasn't a young person, but a person who—dare I say it because I'm not sure of the political correctness—looked like a tiny-eared elf. These days there are all kinds of fantasy movies with weird-looking people, so I don't know why I was surprised. Except how many elves or fairies do we come across in our normal lives?

The person I faced was a female who could vie for Miss Ugly America and probably win. To steal a cliché that is often used in Texas, she looked *rode hard and put away wet.* Though who would have done the deed was hard to imagine—okay, well maybe not these days.

Her obviously-dyed, orange-blonde hair stood out from around her pale face like thorns on a cactus. I sincerely hoped she would have no cause to charge into me. Her nose had a gold ring in one nostril. Hoop earrings, almost as large as her little head, hung down from her ears. I did note that her ears were not totally pointed. Neither was her head. Her lips bore orange lipstick, I guess to match her hair, and she wore a kind of stretchy red muscle shirt thing that revealed boobs that could compete with Dolly Parton's. I didn't know capris came in her size, but I guess they do because she wore some and pink flip flops on her feet.

I can only imagine what my face revealed. I was expecting just about anyone but her. I licked my lips and stuck out my hand, down at her level, and said my name. Her face screwed up in a frown. She didn't take my hand. I let it drop to my side.

"What do you want?" Behind her, were some pieces of living room furniture and a gauzy curtain blowing in an opened window. The wood floor was bare.

I figured I ought to be honest with her. I didn't ask to come in. I didn't want to go in. And she didn't offer. "I've been hired to investigate the murder of Captain Linden, a cruise ship captain who—"

"I knows who he was. So what do you want from me?"

I couldn't fathom why Al hadn't told me what or whom to expect. His idea of a joke, I guess. "Um. I heard you—or someone who lives at this address—might have known him." I'd been expecting a male, but, again, in these modern times, names don't indicate any more than odd faces do.

"I'm not even gonna ask you who told you that, 'cuz I figure you ain't going to tell me anyway."

"Um, no, ma'am." I was beginning to rule out the idea that she could have committed the murder of Captain Linden. I was assuming the ax probably weighed just a bit less than she did, though I hadn't seen it except in pictures.

"Ma'am." She squawked and slapped her leg. "No one has ever called me that before."

"LC," a man's voice called from the back of the house, "who's at the door?"

L and C were not the initials of the person I was supposed to meet. I waited a moment to see whether a warm body would follow up on that question.

"Some woman who is asking about that ship captain's murder a long time ago," she yelled.

From the gloom of the interior, came a portly man I would guess was in his fifties. He had blond-gray hair sticking out almost as bad as the elf's, which made me wonder whether maybe they didn't own a comb. Purple-blue eyes came into focus after the hair. Elongated ears and a triple chin rounded out the picture. Could it be that a circus was in town? He walked to the door with his left hand behind his back and stood so the door concealed his arm. That didn't especially excite me. In his right, he held a floppy slice of pizza.

"Who are you?" He towered over me, being taller up close than he had looked in the distance.

"Mavis Davis, a private investigator."

"Sure." Using the back of his pizza-clasping hand, he scratched his unshaven chin.

I kept my eyes from rolling. "Yes, sir, really. I've been hired to see if I can assist the police in finding Captain Linden's killer. Someone told me there could be someone here who might know something about it."

"Might, might not." He smiled down at LC with teeth than needed a good cleaning.

I wondered what LC stood for. Little Chick? "And your name is?" I still didn't stick out my hand. I had no desire to be touched.

He stuck his chin out. "Mo."

"Nice to meet you, Mo. I'm looking for a man named Axel Waterman." I glanced from his face to hers.

"He in jail," she said.

"Oh." My breath caught. I glanced at her. "Galveston?"

"No, LC," Mo clipped her on the arm, "how many times do I got to tell you he's in prison?"

"Oh." I looked back at him. If I did that a lot, I would have a sore neck later. So prison. Prison is a bit different from jail, though many people get them confused. Whichever it was, both of them had bars. "So…" Questions flew through my head so fast I had to shake myself, at least mentally, to decide which to ask first.

Both of them stared at me. They weren't particularly friendly. On the other hand, they weren't particularly unfriendly. The slightly turned up lips on Mo's face indicated they might have been enjoying themselves. I wasn't, however. No air conditioning blew from inside the apartment. I felt like softened butter approaching a complete meltdown.

"So, what was you going to ask him?" LC said. "Maybe we can answer your questions."

Mo clipped her on the arm again.

"What'd you do that for?" She rubbed her arm and glared up at him. He gave her a wide-eyed look.

"He can't get into no more trouble than he is already, Mo." LC elbowed him in the thigh.

"You going to go to the prison and talk to him?" Mo had been leaning up against the door. He straightened up and bit into his slice.

"Um, depends on where he is."

"Beaumont, last we heard," LC said, looking up at Mo. "Ain't that right?"

"I don't know whether I'll go see him or not." I let out a big sigh. "Do you know what he's in for?"

LC stepped away from Mo. "Smuggling."

This was more like it. Captain Linden could have been involved with that Axel guy. "Like what? Jewelry? Money? What do people smuggle these days?"

"People smuggle people." Mo shook his pizza slice at me and stood with his feet apart.

"Human trafficking," I muttered. My gut wound itself up.

"Yeah, that's it." LC looked up at Mo again. "He was in someplace above Houston and then to Beaumont."

"Humble or Huntsville?"

"Coulda been," Mo said.

"And do you mind telling me how he was smuggling them? I mean, where from?"

"Mexico." Mo maintained his stance.

"What about the Caribbean?" I'm thinking Captain Linden cruised to the Caribbean, right?

"We don't really know for sure, lady." He edged the door toward me. "So we gotta go now."

"Could Axel have been working with Captain Linden? Do you know if Captain Linden could have helped smuggle people into the U.S.?"

They both shrugged. LC said, "He didn't talk about it much, you know what I mean? We all lived here together, us and him and a couple of other guys at one time or so, but most of the time, nobody tells nobody nothing unless there's a reason to."

"And there was no reason for him to tell y'all?"

"Nope." Mo pushed the door forward. "No reason at all."

The last thing I saw was LC's sparkling eyes before Mo closed the door in my face. I was kind of glad because I couldn't help but think there was something in his left hand that he hadn't wanted me to see. I didn't think it was another piece of pizza.

Chapter 14

I DID NOT RUN DOWN THE STAIRS. When I closed the big, heavy door at the bottom of the stairs behind me, I did not run to my car. I maintained my normal clip. Lauren started her car and drove away. I rounded the corner. When I arrived at my own vehicle, I climbed inside and locked it. I've been around the block, figuratively speaking, a couple of times, but those two people had really creeped me out, especially the one I thought might have a gun behind his back.

Lauren pulled up beside me. I was sure I looked like I'd just experienced a traumatic event. I turned the key in the Mustang's ignition, so the air conditioning would come on and put the window down. "Thanks for sticking around."

"You looked so funny when you came out. Did something bad happen?"

"I just met two of the strangest-looking people I've ever seen in my life outside of entertainment venues. Can Albinos have dark eyes, almost black eyes?"

"You saw an albino?"

"She was like a little elf albino, but those eyes of hers didn't look natural. Not that anything about her did. Maybe she wore contacts, though I can't imagine why."

"I really want to hear about this," Lauren said, "but speaking of eyes, I have an eye appointment that I need to get to. Want to come over for dinner tonight?"

I glanced at my watch. "Is this still Monday? It's not like I have anything else on my calendar. What time?" I had a couple of things I could do while it was still early. One of them was to continue my search for John Wayne Linden.

"Six-thirty. You bring the wine. Red. I'm making lasagna."

"Sounds great." I hoped she didn't hear my stomach gurgle in anticipation.

"See you later." Lauren drove to the corner and turned left, again passing in front of the scary house.

Chuck had given me the name of John's friend, so I called him and set up a meeting for thirty minutes later. It didn't take thirty minutes to get anywhere on the island unless way down the West End to the San Luis Pass Bridge. I wasn't going there. John's friend, Tex, lived at the opposite end of town. I stopped at a convenience store for a soft drink before moseying over to where the navigation system on my phone guided me.

Every street in that subdivision bore the name of a fish. Tuna. Albacore. Dolphin. Probably an original idea at the time those little houses were built, which I guessed was probably in the 1950s and 1960s. Most of them were contemporary, modest, one-story homes that showed their age. There were few trees—I'd heard that thousands of trees had drowned in Hurricane Ike—but most lawns were well-kept with shrubs around the front of the houses. Cars filled one-car driveways, overflowing onto the street. I found the fish street and house number Tex had given me and parked in front of the house next door.

Bounding out of the car with the renewed energy the soft drink had given me, I scooted beside the truck in Tex's driveway and pounded on the wood-framed screen door. A man in a wheel chair opened the inside door. He had more than a day's growth of beard and was dressed in a green polo shirt, jeans, and flip flops. Apparently, flip flops were the thing to wear on Galveston Island.

I stuck out my hand. "I'm Mavis Davis. I phoned you a little while ago."

The man gave me the once-over and shook my hand. His shake was better than tepid but not bone-crushing. "Nice to meet you. I'm John Wayne Linden."

I swear I almost wet my pants. I needed to go because of the soft drink I'd guzzled but had been prepared to hold it while I spoke with John Wayne's friend. Faced with the shock of seeing John Wayne in the flesh, my condition had worsened. I'm afraid my pose changed.

"So I guess you want to come in." He frowned but backed up in the wheel chair so I could get by.

I don't know why I didn't hesitate like I had at some other places. Yes, I do. His demeanor wasn't really friendly but not really hostile either. Anyway, I didn't hesitate. I walked past him into a house that smelled of a familiar incense, one frequently burned by pot-smoking folks. "Um, I hate to ask you, but may I use your facilities?"

He raised one eyebrow and snorted like someone who'd been there. "Sure. Down the hall at the end." He pushed the door closed.

Humiliated, but not caring, I almost ran to the loo. While I was there, I did just what any self-respecting PI would do. I looked in the medicine cabinet. That was after I used the WC. And after I washed my hands, of course, though I left the water running so he wouldn't hear the squeak of the medicine cabinet door, if it had one. A squeak, that is. Down on the lowest shelf, stood a bottle with John Wayne's name on it. Hydrocodone. Bearing a recent date, the bottle looked half-full. Next to that, a partially full bottle of tramadol. On the top shelf, stood a spray bottle of naloxone, which I knew was used when there's an overdose. I shut the cabinet door, my mind reeling.

When I returned, John Wayne had rolled his chair into the front room, a smallish living room with light blue walls and blue plaid sofa, love seat, and armchair. On the floor, lay a grayish rag rug with a rectangular coffee table upon it. Matching lamps stood on matching tables on each side of the sofa. If I'd had to, I'd guess someone went to a low-rent furniture store and bought the complete set, probably a man and probably without protest.

"I guess you wanna sit." John Wayne waved a hand at the furniture grouping.

I sat across from him, sinking into soft cushions. "Boy, was I surprised to see you." I held my purse in my lap. My gun was still in the glove box, but he wouldn't know there wasn't some kind of defensive weapon in my purse. Not that I expected any trouble from a man in a wheelchair. I didn't.

"Yeah, it was written all over your face." He still didn't smile. "So, you want to talk about my father's murder, right?"

"Yes, I do. Your Aunt Isley, whom you've probably never heard of because your siblings never heard of her either, hired me to see if I could help the police along."

"That's a nice way of putting it." He clamped his lips together, and his face tightened. He had held his hands loosely in his lap, but they clenched and then relaxed. "Never heard of her either."

"I suppose that's a mystery that might never be solved. Curious, though." And I was curious, as well, about the wheel chair, since Al said John Wayne rode a bike, but I'd wait until later to get to that. "So what can you tell me about the night of your father's murder? What do you remember?"

"You've gotten pretty much the whole story already from what, the police report?"

"Your mother and what your mother told your aunt. And Chuck told me what he knows." His eyes weren't glassy or bloodshot. The pupils weren't constricted or dilated. I realized I didn't know what someone who was on opioids would look like. I didn't get the impression he was on pot or something like that. His speech patterns were okay. He didn't exhibit any behavior other than being a bit irritable.

"Chuck doesn't know much. He wasn't there."

"And Wendy told me about your ax."

"Yeah, she's turned into a real bitch."

I wanted to say *with good cause* but held my tongue. He knew who Wendy was, which meant they'd been in contact—at least since she'd started going by that name. Could that be significant? "But your ax wasn't the murder weapon."

"I don't know why she wanted to go and say that. I did not kill him with my ax." He shook his head several times. "I think she hates me. In fact, I think she hates all of us." His hands rested on the arms of the wheelchair where I couldn't miss them flexing.

"Okay, well Wendy aside, do you mind telling me about the night your father died?"

"I got that ax in Toronto when I was up there one time. I was going to learn how to throw it right and enter contests like the one I saw there." He huffed. "They have contests like that in Las Vegas too. I thought that'd be fun."

"Okay." I knew all that. I wanted to get to the night of the murder.

"The police took it, but they didn't find anything on it because there was nothing to find."

Good grief. Could he shut up about the ax? "So, you want to tell me what happened that night?"

He eyeballed me for a moment and snorted with disgust. "Do I want to? I've only told it a million times. Let's see, my wife and I were upstairs with our baby. We were all asleep. I awoke in a fog. My mother was screaming. I shook Vonnie until she woke up. I ran downstairs and found Mom with blood all over her. I went into the bedroom and found my father. Have you seen the pictures?"

I nodded. "Yeah, pretty nasty."

"That's an understatement." He grimaced.

"John Wayne—is it okay if I call you John Wayne?"

'Sure. Or John. Doesn't matter."

"Well, what I've been wondering is, and I've been out to the house where y'all lived at the time. I know it's huge. How is it possible that you and Vonnie heard nothing until your mother started screaming?" I caught myself leaning forward and forced myself to sit back. I didn't want to appear overeager.

His eyes met mine. "I know it's weird, but it's true. Vonnie and I talked about it a lot—until she left me, that is. But we slept through it." He looked away. "I don't know."

"This is difficult for me to ask, but were you doing drugs then? If you were doing drugs, that might explain why you were sleeping so deeply that you didn't hear anything."

"Someone told you I used to do drugs." His mouth tightened, and he looked over my shoulder. "Yeah, I was, but not that night."

I said nothing, just stared at him, not sure what to believe.

He drew a deep breath. "I didn't do drugs when my father was around. He would have made my mother kick us out of the house."

"And Vonnie?"

"She never touched drugs. She's pretty straight."

"I just can't understand it. Seems like he'd have cried out when he was struck with the ax. I know your mother was knocked out. But if someone came in and struck him with an ax, and he was asleep, wouldn't he have woken up and cried out?"

He shook his head. He was chewing on the inside of his cheek. His hands gripped the arms of the chair. "You think I did it, don't you?"

My chest grew tight, and I reared back. "No. No. I didn't say that."

"But you thought it. Lots of people think I killed my father." His face had turned red. The muscles in his jaws were dancing around.

"I'm just trying to find out what happened."

He backed the wheelchair up and turned sideways to me, in the direction of the front door. I thought he was fixing to throw me out.

"Look, he was a real bastard, but since he wasn't around very much, we all just did the best we could when he was here. We went back to normal when he left again. I didn't have any reason to kill him."

I remembered all the things I'd heard about Captain Linden, some of which would have been plenty of reason to knock the man off, but again, I sat and waited to hear what he'd say next.

He spoke in the direction of the door. "I think the police think the person or persons came and left by boat. There wouldn't have been a car motor to hear if they'd come in a boat. By the time we recovered from our shock enough to wonder where the person was, he was long gone." He sounded like he had his story memorized. Then he turned to me. "I ran out onto the back deck and didn't see anyone."

I could tell I wasn't going to get any more than that out of him. "Okay, John Wayne, thanks for talking to me." I cleared my throat. "Uh—would you mind if I spoke to your ex-wife? And if you don't mind, could you give me her contact info?"

He rolled his eyes to the ceiling. "She's just going to tell you what I just told you."

"I have to cover all the bases. You understand."

"Yeah. Got a pen?"

I pulled out my cell phone. "I'll put it in the little notebook app. Just a second."

He recited Vonnie's email address slowly, so I could punch it into my phone. "I don't know where she lives, except somewhere in Houston. When I go to see Tiffany, we meet at a coffee shop." His eyes met mine. "I only get supervised visitation because of the drugs."

I wasn't surprised. I pitied him. "But if you can prove in the future that you're not doing them—"

"I can get it changed. But I don't have the money to go to court right now." He wheeled his chair toward the front door.

"You're off them now?" I stood and put my phone in my purse. Evidently, it was time for me to leave.

He slapped his leg. "Ever since I broke my leg."

"Oh, wow. Drugs have something to do with that?"

"Yep. I was high and got hit by a car on my bicycle." He shook his head. "It was dark. And yeah, I did some stupid stuff." He shook his head and moved the chair closer to the door. "Could have died. They talk in N.A. about hitting bottom. That was mine. When I left the hospital, I swore I'd never touch them again."

That's why the hydrocodone bottle wasn't empty. He'd toughed it out. Or so he said. Maybe he thought he could sell me on that story, and he was really still doing them, and what was in the bottle was a refill.

I skirted around the chair and pulled the front door open. "Thanks for talking with me." I held my hand out, and he shook it. "Take care, John."

When I reached my car and drove away, his words were still echoing. *"I did not kill him with my ax."*

Chapter 15

I TOOK LAUREN UP ON HER OFFER of dinner, without even stopping by my room. I had emailed Vonnie and hadn't heard back, so I phoned Margaret from the car and asked her to do an Internet search. If she found her, I could run up to Houston to do the interview.

Lauren greeted me at the door, holding her dog back by its collar. "Frisky, sit." The shepherd sat next to her leg. "You can come in. He won't bite you. Hold out your hand."

The air in her house smelled of spicy tomatoes, kind of like the scary house but without the weed. My stomach growled. I glanced from her to the dog's face. She'd become a pretty good friend in a short period of time, so I had to trust her. My hand crept toward Frisky. When my hand was in biting range, Frisky sniffed at it like it was a dead animal. I didn't move. Lauren was grinning. I gave her a faux smile and, when Frisky licked my hand, a real one. She released her hold on the dog's collar, but Frisky only sniffed at me, no biting. His sniffs were rather intrusive, but I stood there and tolerated him until Lauren called him down. After a minute or two, he and I were fast friends.

Lauren made good on her promise of lasagna. I love pasta. It loves me too. Sticks to my hips, my thighs, my…

"I figure the weird little woman's name was either Elsie or L.C.," I said between bites of lasagna. "I thought about it, and if it's L.C., I think it stands for Little Chick. People like that usually don't go by their given names. They use street names."

Lauren wore white short shorts. Really short. And a pale pink, almost-white, V-neck T-shirt. She could pull it off. Wearing that skimpy outfit, I mean, not literally taking off her clothes. Not sure I could. I hardly ever wear anything shorter than jeans that go to the top of my shoes. She kept the air conditioning in her house just above freezing. I didn't see how she could stand it. I was thinking of asking to borrow a sweater.

She refilled my wine glass and poured some for herself. "I heard that enough times in court. So often witnesses didn't even know the real name of the person they were testifying about."

"If I never have to go to another house with people like that living in it, it'll be too soon." I put another fork full of lasagna in my mouth and followed it with a gulp of wine. The tomato sauce was sweet but not too sweet. The red wine was a bit bitter but went well with the pasta.

"But you know you will. Want some more lasagna?" She scooped some onto her plate, still leaving a lot for me if I wanted it.

"I'm approaching stuffed. Thanks for backing me up today, Lauren. If I'd been in Houston, I'd have gotten Margaret or Candy to be my 'lookout.'"

"Hey, no prob. Have you heard back from Margaret yet?"

I had brought Lauren up to date about the call. "Probably won't 'til tomorrow. I really don't want to run back up there but will if I have to."

Lauren cut her food into small pieces. After putting her knife down, she didn't need to pick it up again. I wondered why she did that but didn't ask.

"I've been wondering something, Mavis. If you don't mind telling me."

"Anything."

Her eyes waltzed. "Have you figured out who did it yet? Who killed Captain Linden?"

I laughed. "If I had, I wouldn't have to drive up to Houston and talk to Vonnie."

"You don't think she did it, do you?"

"No. I don't think a lady with a baby left her child and went downstairs and found an ax from someplace and chopped up her father-in-law. But now that you mention it, I've heard so many bad things about the man, I'm beginning to wonder whether he did something to her that would give her a motive."

"Like what are you thinking?"

"I'm not really thinking anything. At least, I wasn't. But now my brain is rushing around my head looking at various possibilities." I patted my stomach. I could just about finish what was left on my plate without bursting.

"Maybe she knows who did it. Ever think of that?" Lauren pushed her plate away and sat back.

"Like her husband, John Wayne?" I had wondered about that. John was a real possibility.

"He could have, right? I mean, you talked to him. I didn't. Do you think he did it?"

"He was using drugs then. He could have been high on something, and then something set him off, maybe something his father said before his parents went out to dinner." In that case, where did he get an ax all of a sudden?

"Premeditated murder. He planned it while they were out." She picked up her wine glass. "The sun's starting to set, so it's cooler outside. Let's go sit on the deck."

I glanced at the dirty dishes on the table, thinking I should offer to help clean up, but it was her house, her kitchen, and I'm sure she had a dishwasher, so I merely followed her outside. We sank into Adirondack chairs that faced the Gulf. Frisky settled down between our chairs. A strong salt breeze blew our hair. Gray-green choppy waves washed ashore. Even with the humidity, I was comfortable after I peeled off my blazer. While watching the breakers, I wondered whether there was a solution to such a stale case as the Linden murder. Should I have taken the case at all? Or should I have discouraged Isley from pursuing it? If I couldn't find the killer, could she be satisfied just learning about the family, about her long-lost relatives?

"What are you thinking?" Lauren lay back in her chair, her feet propped up on a footstool of sorts that was made to match the turquoise chair in which she sat.

Trying not to sigh too loudly, I glanced at her. "This whole situation and whether I should have even gotten myself into this."

She slurped her wine. "Look at it this way. If you hadn't, you wouldn't have ever met me. How about that?"

"That's true. And I'm glad I did." Three brown pelicans flew toward the water and plopped down with small splashes.

"So, it's getting to you? You've been on the case for not even a week, right?"

I nodded. "And working my tail off."

"What have you found out? You said John Wayne may have had a motive. And he had opportunity if his mother and his wife would have covered for him."

"Yeah. Chuck had motive too." I had told her about Chuck over dinner. We agreed that Captain Linden might have deserved to die for all the abuse he heaped on people, but that didn't get us closer to who did it. "But I don't think Wendy would have done it."

"There's that man who's in prison. Someone connected to him, then, if not him. What are you going to do about him?"

I took a chance and patted Frisky. He smiled at me. At least I think that's what it was. He didn't growl or move away. "That's a good one. I sure as heck don't want to go see the guy in prison on the off chance he might give me some clue as to what all was going on with him and the captain, and whether the captain did something to him he deserved to die for."

"Uh, I think I understand what you're saying." She stared out at the ocean. "I'd hate to think Roxanne would have been capable of doing it. When she lived next door, she seemed pretty nice, the little I knew her."

"Of course, you didn't know her back then. Maybe she was different somehow." We exchanged glances. Her wrinkled brow reflected what I was feeling.

"But would a woman be strong enough to wield an ax that many times and do that much damage? I have a hard time believing that," Lauren said.

"There was a case thirty or forty years ago in a small town where a woman axed another woman to death. And then there was…"

"Enough said. I don't need to hear about every ax murder you happen to know about."

I grinned. "Okay, but anyway, with a sharp enough ax, it wouldn't be too hard."

"True, but still…did she hit herself in the head?" Lauren sort of snorted out a laugh.

"Yeah, no. She could have, if she's really nuts. I couldn't see Wendy armed with an ax, throwing open the door, and running in and doing the deed, either. That's why I'm stymied."

"Wait. Wait. Wait. What about Roxanne's boyfriend? The one you said looks like a platypus."

That was a thought. But had Roxanne been hooked up with him then? I didn't think so. I sipped at my wine. "Wish you had lived here when the murder happened. Then you could tell me whether you ever saw Puss-face here while the captain was out of town. But you didn't, so you can't."

She laughed. "Right. Is there a way to find out when they got together? And if they'd been together then? Wouldn't one of the sons have told you if they knew? Wouldn't they have told the police? That was a long time ago, and I have a hard time believing she could have been with, what'd you call him, Puss-face? And no one knew about it."

"Yeah. It doesn't seem feasible. I guess I have to keep on looking." My cell made a noise then. I tapped on it. A text from Margaret. *You can meet Vonnie tomorrow morning at 9:30.* I glanced at Lauren. "It's Margaret, my assistant."

"What'd she say? You can see Vonnie or not?"

"I can, but I sure don't want to drive back up there. If there were only another way to find out if Vonnie knows anything worth the drive."

"You'll at least be able to give her the once over. See if you think she could have done it."

"All this discussin' and still no idea of a solution." An enormous sigh escaped me. Three women. Three men. And no way to narrow it down. Yet.

Chapter 16

TUESDAY MORNING, I AWOKE EARLY TO the cry of seagulls. I dragged myself out of bed, my eyes open only a crack, and pulled the drapes back to see if I could figure out why the birds were so loud. There hadn't been that racket any of the other days. The black and white birds circled in the air and dove toward a balcony not far from mine. I opened the sliding glass door and stuck only my head out, since I wore no pjs. An adolescent boy dressed only in swim trunks and a toddler dressed only in a plastic diaper were taking turns throwing balled up pieces of what looked like white bread into the air for the birds. Yuck, white bread. I never touch the stuff myself, but I guess seagulls aren't so picky.

I let the curtain drop back. Squinting at the clock, I saw it was almost time to get up anyway. With the never-ending construction on Interstate 45, there was no easy way to get into Houston to meet Vonnie. I had no gyrocopter, so I'd have to sit in bumper-to-bumper traffic. I stopped the alarm on my phone and crawled into the shower. Thirty minutes later, I was in said traffic with a coffee cup, almost as big as an urn, in-between my legs and an egg sandwich made with stone ground wheat bread, not that white stuff, in my hand. I had allowed plenty of time to find the coffee shop Vonnie had designated as our meeting place. I assumed the shop was the same one where she met John Wayne for his periods of visitation, not that it mattered.

Turns out, Vonnie bore a striking resemblance to John's mother. Some people might say they were the same phenotype, similar build, facial shape, nose, though hair color was different. Vonnie's was blond and curly whereas Roxanne was a brunette. Some people might worry over the psychological ramifications of John Wayne marrying a woman with similar characteristics to his mother. Not me. I had no need to spend my time thinking of that stuff.

Vonnie called to me when I entered the shop. She told me Margaret had told her to watch for a tall red head. I put out my hand, and she shook it, her grip firm. I know, I know, you'd think by now I'd conclude a person's handshake really doesn't mean anything, but no. I maintain that the touch, the feel, the moistness, and a few other factors gave out clues about a person, though I'm not always sure what. Anyway, after shaking her hand, I stepped to the counter and ordered still another coffee. The place wasn't busy. By nine-thirty, most people had gotten their coffee and gone to work.

"So, Vonnie, you know why I'm here, right?" I sipped and stared at her face for any telltale indications that might mean something. That's what private investigators are supposed to do, right? I think it's in the rulebook. Maybe Rule 34?

Her lips were pressed tightly together, and her forehead scrunched up. She nodded and rocked side to side, her shoulders and torso moving as though to the beat of some music. I'd had enough of weird people after meeting the two at the scary house the day before. More, I didn't need.

I guess she saw me set my cup down and study her because she laughed and said, "I love that song."

I hadn't even heard the music. Could I be more intense than I thought? "You had me worried for a minute." I glanced at my watch. "Are you on the clock or in any kind of a hurry?"

"I'm on a break, but I have time to talk." She tossed her head. "So John Wayne sent you?"

"Not really, his Aunt Isley. And I know what you're going to say. You didn't know he had an aunt."

"I didn't. Where's she been all these years?" She fidgeted with the handle of her coffee mug.

"In the military. Apparently, she and her brother were estranged over something she really couldn't define. She's ill, terminal. She wants me to, uh, help the police figure out who killed Skip."

"Who cares?" She pulled a face. "Well, I guess this Isley person does, but I'd be surprised if anyone else did. He was a mean, creepy sort of person."

"Really? Creepy?"

"Yeah. When he was out in public—like if the family went together somewhere—which we seldom did—he was like a different person, all smiles and congenial. But he wasn't that way at home." She chewed on her lower lip.

"I've heard a lot of things about him from all three of the children. Do you mind sharing what you know?"

She shrugged, as if it didn't matter now. "He was pretty bad. It didn't take long for me to see what was going on after John Wayne and I got together. Captain Linden was the reason they're all screwed up."

"All?" I sipped from my coffee but kept my eyes on her.

"Well," she dipped her head down and looked up at me, "Hanna Beth might be okay now that she's been gone so long. If she got counseling or something."

"Chuck's an alcoholic," I said with a sidelong glance at her. "You knew that?"

"His drug of choice. Alcohol was more acceptable with the crowd he hung out with than street drugs."

"You also knew he was gay?" In response, she raised her eyebrows. I said, "Did everyone know he was gay except his father?"

"Pretty much, yeah. Nobody cared one way or the other. Nobody made a big deal out of it." She ran her forefinger around the lip of the mug.

"So their mother knew about it?"

She nodded. "But she never told their father. She tried to act like she didn't know when he confronted her, but after he slapped her around a few times, she admitted she'd known for quite a while."

I winced. "You were there the night he humiliated Chuck in front of his friends?"

"Well, we were back at the house when they came home." She stared down at the table. "We tried to stay out of his way until he left on another cruise."

I rested my elbows on the table and my chin in my hands, covering my mouth, the expletives remaining unsaid. She crossed her arms and put her shoulders back. "I figured you knew all this."

"Some of it. Mrs. Linden isn't that forthcoming."

She raised one eyebrow. "No surprise there."

I'd already figured that Roxanne either stayed with the captain because she was afraid to leave, or she stayed for the money. When I was growing up, my mother had a friend who stayed for the money. At least that's what my mother had said. "So what about John Wayne? I know he did drugs a lot."

"Like all the time. I had to get Tiffany and me away from him."

"Was he using the night his father was killed?"

"He swears he wasn't, but I know he had some qua." She swallowed what was left of her coffee and pushed the mug aside.

"Quaaludes?

"Yeah and was drinking some of the tequila his father had brought back."

"He could've passed out just from enough tequila. What about you?"

"Not me. I had to take care of Tiffany. I had to wake up if she cried in the night. I couldn't trust John Wayne to."

"Yet, you didn't wake up when Captain Linden was being murdered."

She drew a deep breath and looked past my shoulder. She cracked her knuckles.

"You didn't wake up, did you? That's what the police report says. Vonnie?"

She swallowed, a really visible swallow. She ran her fingers over her mouth, leaving two fingers across her lips.

I leaned toward her and pulled her hand away from her mouth. "You heard it?"

She sighed. Her eyes met mine. "I heard screams. I thought Captain was beating Roxanne again."

"You'd heard that before?"

"I just said so, didn't I?" She rubbed her lips together. "It sounded different, somehow. Scary. Scarier than ever."

"You didn't go down there? You didn't see who did it?"

"Hell, no. I pulled the covers over my head at first, then I thought I should wake up John Wayne, so I shook him. I shook him a lot. He was slow to wake up—that's why I think he was doing some quas or something." Fear filled her eyes.

If I recalled correctly, John Wayne had said he woke her up, not the other way around. I wondered whether that meant anything. "I don't blame you for not going down there. Had you ever tried to help out Roxanne before?"

"I started to once. I started to go downstairs the first time I heard it—right after we moved in with her, them, but John Wayne said not to. He pulled me back."

I wondered whether John Wayne had ever tried to defend his

mother. Or if Chuck had. Anyway…that was a moot point. "So, what happened? John Wayne finally woke up?"

"He was real groggy, but when he heard a scream coming from the bottom of the stairs, his mother's scream, he became more alert. He scrambled out of bed and flung open the door and ran to where she was, collapsed on the bottom step."

"And you were with him? The baby was still asleep? She didn't wake up, so you went down with him?"

She rubbed her hands together like they were cold, and she was trying to warm them. She put them to her mouth and moved them away. Her eyes searched my face. She finally said, "I may as well tell you. I thought I heard something outside. I ran to the window and looked out. I didn't know who it was, but I saw someone I thought was a man running toward the dunes in the dark."

While I was still digesting our conversation, Vonnie excused herself, saying she had to get back to work. Clearly, she wasn't interested in staying and 'splainin.' If I wanted to get more out of her, I would have to track her down another time. I watched her back as she disappeared into the crowds populating the sidewalk. Why'd she been so forthcoming? Could I trust what she'd said? I wasn't so sure.

I literally hot-footed it back to my Mustang, the temperature being almost 100 degrees, and headed back to Galveston. On the way there, I again stopped by the ME's office in Texas City, where they actually had my copy of the autopsy, including photos, ready for pickup. After that, I drove to an office supply place where I stood by while the young man behind the counter scanned the multi-paged autopsy report and emailed it to Isley. That done, I downed some greasy-spoon enchiladas at a Mexican restaurant, and no sooner had I climbed back into my car before my cell beeped, indicating I had a message. And not just one. Isley had apparently been texting, emailing, and phoning me for the past hour. I, wanting to avoid any more indigestion than the enchiladas would give me, had turned off my phone until after I finished my meal.

The next time it chirped, I clicked on. "Mavis Davis." I could already see it was Isley.

"This report's supposed to be on my brother?" Isley barely got those words out before she coughed long and hard into the phone. I held mine away from my ear until she stopped. "I can't hardly make out his face except to see that he's a white man with the right coloring. There's a small checkerboard pattern across the copy—the whole page."

"The boy behind the counter probably scanned it on a pdf setting instead of jpeg. Can you read the text? And what about the other photos? The ones of the body?" I hated thinking about them myself, what with his torso being all chopped up by that ax. Enchiladas, blood, and guts didn't mix very well. I suppressed a burp.

"All the pictures have that checkerboard. They're not very clear." Her ragged breath, though, came across clearly.

"I'm so sorry. I'll get you some better copies when I get a minute." I went ahead and started my car to get the air-conditioning on. I didn't want to die of heat exhaustion, which could easily happen in a closed-up car in South Texas in the summer.

"What I can see is disgusting. I mean, he scanned it on a black and white scanner, thank goodness. I didn't really want to see all those bloody chopping marks."

Or the cavernous gaps between the chops, I bet. The gaps in the decedent's flesh had closed up but still, his body was a ghastly sight. "I know what you mean."

She coughed again, really hard. Sounded like she was continuing to get worse.

"Mavis, I haven't seen him in decades. I don't know what I expected. I guess I thought he'd look like he did the last time I saw him, but he doesn't look right, what I can see of him."

"What do you mean?" I dabbed at my forehead and the back of my neck with a tissue. The perspiration had been quick to start on the way back to my car.

"Like where is the scar on the top of his foot?"

"The top of his foot? Can you see the top of his foot clearly?"

"He had a scar on the top of his foot from where he shot himself in the foot with a spear gun when we were kids. He used to swim around Offats Bayou with his spearfishing gun. Our parents gave it to him for, I think it was, his eleventh birthday. Stupidly, I remember thinking at the time."

I'd agree with that.

"Anyway, he was playing with it and shot himself in the foot."

Some of my muscles flexed, and they weren't the ones in my arms.

"When the doctor got the head of the spear out of the top of Charles' foot, it left a jagged scar. I don't see that on the top of either foot of the dead man in the photos here."

Either foot? I wasn't going to point out that she was saying it was only one foot—not that he somehow shot through both feet, but whatever. "But the checkerboard could be obscuring it, right? I mean, the feet were taken at a distance. You're looking at a photo of the entire torso from what, head to foot, and the feet are the farthest distance from the camera lens? Add that to the checkerboard problem...plus he's grown since then. The scar wouldn't look the same."

She was quiet on the other end.

"And hey, why are we talking about a scar on the top of his foot, anyway?"

She cleared her throat. "I don't know. In a way, I guess I just don't want this dead man to be my brother."

"I understand." If I'd had a brother, I wouldn't want him to be chopped up either, unless he'd done something egregious to me when we were kids.

After we hung up, I drove over arched causeway bridge, admiring the view of the island from the air. Galveston looked like a flat piece of terrain just floating on the sparkling water. To my right, several small boats were leaving a wake in their path. A couple of specks of land protruded into the channel. To my left, were the outbound bridge and the railroad bridge on the other side of it. In the distance, tall smokestacks and pipes rose from the ground. Those would be the refineries and chemical plants. A few houses dotted the shoreline on the mainland side. Rough old houses up on pilings, porches overlooking the bay. Various styles of boats traversed the waters there, as well. Salt air permeated my car. A kind of euphoria filled me as I crossed the bridge's peak and headed down the other side.

I thought of Isley, who knew she was terminally ill, imagining that a corpse in a morgue couldn't be her brother, as if she could will him back to life. A twinge of sadness tweaked my heart. Poor, pathetic, lonely, dying woman. Desperate to find out about him. To have a connection with him and his family before she departed this earth. She didn't have anyone else.

On the other hand, my pragmatic side said, *"Why not at least go speak to the widow Linden and ask about the scar?"* It wouldn't hurt to have a casual conversation just to express Isley's concern. And to confirm for Isley that yes, it was her brother, to set Isley's mind at ease. Though I wished in a way that it weren't, after all I'd learned about him. I'd been paid to find out who killed the man and to do a bit of a background on the rest of the family. But did that mean I had to tell the grieving sister that her brother was some kind of sociopathic monster, some mad man? Because that's what I thought he must have been. From what everyone had said, he thought of no one but himself and cared only that whatever the wife and kids did would not reflect badly on him.

My waning hours, midafternoon, found me parking in front of Roxanne's house in mid-town Galveston. I should have stopped at a coffee shop, but since I hadn't, I hoped she'd offer me some coffee or at least some tea. Maybe even a couple of toothpicks to hold my eyelids open.

After banging on the door, I stood on the porch, thankful there was an overhang, and looked up and down the street. No one was about. Why would they be in that heat and humidity? I admired the houses and gardens and thought that if, in my wildness dreams, there was a way I could move down to Galveston, I would have a difficult choice to make. Condo on the beach overlooking the Gulf of Mexico? Condo in downtown Galveston where art galleries, boutiques, and coffee shops lined the streets? Or a home in one of the older neighborhoods with mature oaks, fascinating architecture from another era, and quiet ambiance? Houston was so loud most of the time. A quiet neighborhood was attractive to me.

Finally, Roxanne opened the door. Her disheveled hair, wrinkled T-shirt, capris, and bare feet told me that if she hadn't been napping, she at least had been resting and not expecting company.

"Miss Davis," she said, not quite warmly. "I hadn't expected to see you again so soon."

Probably what she meant was that she had hoped she'd never see me again. I hadn't gotten the impression last time I was there that I'd be welcomed back like a long lost relative.

"Sorry to disturb. You look like maybe you were resting? May I come in?" I put my foot on the threshold in hopes that she would let me inside and not close the door on it.

She stood back and opened the door wider, so I could come through. Once inside, I thought I'd push my luck. "Could I trouble you for a cup of coffee or tea? I have the same issues you appear to have. A feeling of fatigue in the middle of the afternoon."

She closed the door and walked past me, putting herself between me and the kitchen, and crossed her arms. "Is this some kind of a ploy or something?"

"No. What?" I shook my head. "Seriously, I haven't been sleeping well. I have a hard time staying awake in the middle of the afternoon. I don't sleep well when I travel—at least not for the first few days."

"And you couldn't go to a coffee shop?"

"I could have, but I wanted to talk to you about something. So could I have a cup of something or not?" I could feel my eyelids drooping.

She rolled her eyes. "I'll make you something. Come in the kitchen."

I followed her and sat down at her little kitchen table. She dug around in a canister and pulled out one of those pod thingies and popped it into one of those machines that I had wanted to buy but had decided I didn't want to spend my hard-earned money on. She poured water and stood next to the machine and looked at me. I looked back. We didn't speak. I was hoping for a cookie or two also.

Within a few minutes, she placed a cup of coffee in front of me and started one of her own. When hers was done, she sat across from me and heaved a loud sigh. "Okay. Now, what did you want to talk to me about?"

I'd sipped from my cup and was feeling a little better, more alert. The sugar from a cookie could have improved on that, but it was not to be. I took another sip. "I was able to get a copy of your husband's autopsy. Have you seen it?"

She was swallowing some coffee and gulped almost audibly. "God, no. I don't understand why you would want to see it either."

"I didn't. Isley did. I got it for her and sent it to her late this morning."

"Okay. And?"

"Do you want to see it?"

She shook her head. "No. Why would I? I saw the body."

"True. Isley had some questions about it, and I thought if you looked at the autopsy, you might be able to answer her questions."

A noise came from the front of the house. The front door opened, and a man called out, "Roxanne!"

Roxanne's face became more of a mask than it already had been. "In the kitchen."

Footsteps slapped the wood floor, and Platypus-face appeared in the kitchen doorway. *I* gulped almost audibly then. I knew it was him right away because even having only seen him from a distance, his face was easily recognizable.

He smiled at Roxanne for just a moment before seeing me. Then he grinned at me. "Hello there," he said in one of the deepest and most melodious voices I'd ever heard. He could have been a deejay. His smile grew wider. "I didn't realize you had company, Roxanne. Shall I come back another time?"

Roxanne shook her head. "Not at all. Mavis, this is Jeffrey Downs. Jeffrey, this is Mavis Davis. She's the one I told you about who is looking into Skip's murder."

Puss-face, who now that I had a chance to see him up close, I decided looked more like Rumpole of the Bailey because of his huge, red, veiny nose, put out his hand and said, again in that charming voice, "Oh-h-h, so nice to meet you. How are you finding Galveston?"

I stood and took a few steps toward him and shook his hand. He was about as tall as I, but really thin, wiry-like, and his sweaty hand almost slipped out of mine. "Nice to meet you too. And I have loved Galveston for a long time. Used to come down here when I was a kid with my mother and go to beach. And my...uh...boyfriend and I come down to the beach sometimes, but this trip, I'm really seeing a different side of it." Why was I rattling on to this man like he was my new best friend?

"Jeffrey and I went to high school together," Roxanne said.

"I thought you grew up in California." I went back to my chair and sat down, wanting to finish that good coffee even if I wasn't going to get a cookie.

"We did," they both said at the same time and laughed. Jeffrey pulled up a chair and sat down, too. "Want to make me a cup, too, hon?"

"We went to our high school reunion a few years ago and found out we both lived in Galveston." I couldn't tell whether Roxanne's smile was real or faux. She started a cup for him and returned to the table.

Jeffrey laughed again. "Isn't that funny?" He had deep-set dimples.

I nodded, watching the two of them over the top of my cup. What I thought was funny was this man with the big nose. Funny-looking, I mean. Though he was rail thin, he had several double chins. He was dressed in a cotton, long-sleeved shirt and chinos and wore running shoes. Long-sleeved shirt in the summer? What was that about?

Roxanne said, "Yeah, we got to talking and couldn't believe it. We've been best friends ever since."

"When was that?" I asked, wondering whether Etta knew about the friendship. Not that I was going to mention it, at least not to them. I didn't even want him or them to know I knew Etta. And I wondered whether Roxanne knew Etta or *of* Etta? And was their relationship more than just a friendship? I knew some folks of opposite sexes who were pretty much best friends, so I knew it was possible. I couldn't help but think about how Etta had said Jeffrey was off selling pharmaceuticals so much of the time. Was he really? Or not?

"At the thirtieth year reunion. A couple of years ago." Jeffrey got up and got his own cup from the coffee-maker thingy and fixed it the way he liked it.

"Oh, huh. Strange how things happen." It occurred to me that by all appearances, Etta was a good deal older than Rumpole. I could assign several motives to him marrying an older woman. "Anyway, Roxanne, I did want to talk to you about the autopsy. I can get my copy out of the car if you want. And then I'll get out of your hair."

"Ugh. No. What is it that Isley wants to know? I can't imagine. Can you, Jeffrey?"

He turned back toward us. "I'm afraid I came in too late to know what's going on," he said in that smooth voice, his dimples showing as he smiled again.

"Apparently Isley has seen Skip's autopsy and has some questions."

"Well, she's only seen an emailed copy," I said, "but she thinks the body doesn't look like what she thinks it should."

Roxanne shook her head. "I don't understand."

Jeffrey was sitting between us, his head turning from me to Roxanne and back again.

"Okay, the guy who scanned it in must have done something wrong because my copy is really good, even though it's a photocopy, but the scanned copy is like on a checkerboard background or something like that."

"But she can tell from her copy that something is not right?" Jeffrey asked.

"I think she's just hoping. She's been estranged from her brother for years and years, and I think she'd like to think there was some mistake." Now that Jeffrey was sitting in close proximity to me, my nose twitched from his body odor, a sour, fetid smell. I guess the heat caused him to sweat a lot.

"But the ME said the autopsy report you received was for my husband, right?" Roxanne said.

"Yes. So anyway, Isley's main point is that she says there should be a scar on the top of the decedent's foot where he shot a spear into it from a spear gun when he was about eleven or twelve years old. She doesn't see a scar in the photograph that's of his whole body." I looked from one to the other of them.

"I didn't know him," Jeffrey said, "so I wouldn't know, but wouldn't a scar have smoothed over somewhat after thirty or forty years?"

"That's what I said, but I wanted to ask you, Roxanne, just to reassure Isley." I drained the rest of my coffee and set the cup aside.

"I don't know, Mavis." Her brow wrinkled up. "I really don't remember. Does anyone really examine her husband's feet?"

I stifled a snicker. "I wouldn't know, but I know I haven't examined my boyfriend's."

"Wouldn't there be hair growing on the top of his feet? A little hair anyway," Jeffrey said. "I know I have some."

That was TMI for me.

"I really couldn't tell you one way or the other." Roxanne rubbed her cheek and rested her chin in her palm. "What else did she wonder about?"

"She didn't articulate much else. She didn't think he looked right, his face, but admitted people change over the years. Then she said she guessed she was thinking he'd look like he did the last time she saw him."

"Poor lady," Jeffrey said.

Roxanne shook her head. "I identified the body for the police. You know, that official identification you have to do—even after they came to my house and all. I know it was him."

I stood. "Well, that's all. I'm sorry to bother you, but I felt I had to ask. Thanks for the coffee. It perked me up."

Roxanne walked me to the door and opened it for me.

"Thanks again, Roxanne," I said and then louder, "Goodbye, Jeffrey. Take care."

As I was walking to my car, I realized Roxanne hadn't unlocked the door for me when I left. Had she locked it behind me when she let me in? Did she always leave the door unlocked? Was the neighborhood that safe? Had the door been unlocked when Jeffrey came in? Or did Jeffrey have a key? If he had a key, then I could assume they were friends, right? Friends with benefits or more than that? And how long had that been going on?

Chapter 17

WHILE MY BRAIN WAS THICK WITH questions, my cell phone rang. Lauren wanted to meet me for an early dinner. We agreed to the Gumbo Bar in half an hour. She gave me directions, and I realized I'd walked right past it the other day on my way to those condos, The Lofts, when I'd parked by the Opera House and the parking lot the condo owners used.

The aroma of seafood and spices slapped me in the face when I entered Little Daddy's Gumbo Bar, which could be called a hole in the wall but is much more than that. The restaurant has tables out on the sidewalk, and the inside is a shotgun-shaped place—a long narrow room with a bar halfway down one side, booths opposite, and toward the back, a square dining area with four-top wooden tables and chairs with lime green seat covers. The walls are red brick, this being the historic district with original structures dating back over a hundred years, and big flat screen TVs were spaced out high on the wall behind the bar and dining area, and paintings that I can only describe as modern weird. I'm not much into modern art, but I would only buy one of them if I wanted to wake up thinking I was in Salvador Dali's studio or in a Hieronymus Bosch nightmare. At least, that's what I thought then. I stand to be corrected.

During the time before she arrived, I looked over their expansive beer list. In my humble opinion, Americans are given too many choices. I'd say there were at least fifty different beers on that list, light ones, dark ones, those in pink-labeled bottles and blue-labeled bottles. How's a girl supposed to decide? The only problem was I didn't have enough time to try them all. So I chose a longneck in a pink-labeled bottle. By the time Lauren arrived, I'd finished that and had moved on from a blue-labeled bottle to a yellow-labeled bottle.

"I thought you liked wine." Lauren slung her shoulder bag, followed by her body, into the booth across from where I sat leaning forward what you could almost call morosely and staring at the alligator on the wall.

"I like wine, but I confess to a propensity for beer when I'm feeling befoodled."

"Befoodled?" She signaled the waiter.

"I just made that up." I took another swig of my longneck.

"A light beer on tap," she told the waiter, a thin, dark-haired Italian-looking guy, "and as soon as you can, we'll order."

Lauren wore all white—white capris, white ruffled cotton blouse, white-framed sunglasses, and I bet if I looked under the table, I'd see white sandals. Even her earrings were silver with little white painted seagulls on them. Or some kind of bird. "You look duded up." I scooted my chair closer to the table.

"When I leave the house in the summer, I wear white. That's my rule. It's hot as hell out there." She took the beer from the waiter and blew the head off it followed by a long, almost-silent slurp. "Mmm." She smiled up at him. "I'll have the Mumbo-Gumbo."

"Yes, ma'am. The one with everything but the kitchen sink?" His eyes twinkled when he smiled at her. He turned to me. "And you?"

I hadn't noticed who'd been bringing my beer. Could have been him. I'd been in a little world of my own. "Sausage and chicken gumbo," I said. I hadn't looked at the menu, but every gumbo place had sausage and chicken. "No, wait, seafood?" What was I thinking? I was in Galveston.

"Yes, ma'am." He left.

Was it my imagination, or did his voice have a not-as-friendly-as-it-had-been-to-Lauren tone?

"You look sort-of off somehow," Lauren said and took another sip from the frosted mug.

"Yeah. I am. I'm getting nowhere with this case."

"You've only been on it what, four days? Give yourself a break. Every time I talk to you, you've been out seeing someone new."

"If you count last Friday, five days, if you count today too." I was beginning to feel better. Was it the three beers? The fact that Lauren had shown up? The smell of seafood? "But I feel like by now, I should have something concrete to show poor Isley."

"Rome etcetera." She stared at me, her lips curling into a smile. "What've you been doing today?"

"Oh, and that's another thing." I slammed my palm on the table top and sat up straighter. "I met Rumpole of the Bailey."

She laughed. "O—kay. And that's who?"

"When Roxanne lived next door to you, did she ever have a visitor with a yellow BMW?"

"Oh, yeah, not a becoming color for a BMW. Looked like a not-quite-ripe lemon on four wheels."

"Well, I'd seen him before." I wasn't sure whether I should tell her exactly where. "And now I've met him."

"That's Rumpole of the Bailey? I'm glad I've always been a PBS fan."

"Right. Well, I had that other name for him, but now that I've seen him up close, that's who he reminds me of." I huffed out a deep breath, feeling even better. I took another long swallow of beer, wishing I had a cigarette—addict that I am—but I'd quit some time ago, so I had to be satisfied with deep breathing. "Except this guy isn't a tub of lard like Rumpole of the Bailey was. At least, that's how I remember him, Rumpole not the Rumpole look-alike."

"I think you're making sense, but I'm not sure."

"The person driving that lemon BMW, what did he look like?"

"Well, yeah, a man. Balding with that gray fringe around his head like they all have. I couldn't tell for sure, but I suspect a comb-over. I only saw him climbing the stairs once. The other times not so close."

"Did he have a big nose? A Rumpole nose?"

"Now that you mention it—"

"Same guy." I banged my bottle down, some beer splashing out.

"Well, it would have to be. How many people could have such poor taste in car colors?"

"And kind of ugly with several chins and poor taste in clothes? Almost wiry thin, but I couldn't help but think, because of his chins, that he must have been obese at one time?"

"Must be the same person. You saw him today?" Lauren pushed a paper napkin toward the spill from my bottle.

"Met him today."

She sat back. "Where?"

"At Roxanne's."

"No way." Lauren shook he head.

"Way."

"Why were you at Roxanne's?"

A different waiter came and set our bowls in front of us. Scoops of white rice like two fat cheeks sat on top of the gumbos. The aroma caused my mouth to water. Without either of us saying anything, we both picked up our spoons and took our first bites.

I almost spit mine out. "Hot." I fanned my mouth. I swallowed and chased that mouthful of soup with a swig of beer. "Think I'll wait a minute or two for it to cool down." I pushed the clumps of rice into the gumbo and stirred.

Lauren nodded. "Mine's hot but not burning hot. Go on. Tell." She took another bite.

I put my shoulders back, so I wouldn't be hovering over the bowl like a vulture. "Okay, so I dropped by Roxanne's to tell her that Isley had some questions about the autopsy photos."

"You sent her copies? Isley?"

"Yes, but the goofball who sent them at the office supply store didn't do it right, and they had some kind of checkerboard across them. Isley thought something was off anyway."

She stopped and looked at me.

"Oh, and I wasn't the goofball. The guy behind the counter."

She laughed. "What did she think was wrong?"

"His foot should have had a scar on it where he shot himself with a spear gun when they were kids."

"Ouch. Bet that hurt."

I tasted my gumbo. The gravy only. Spicy and not too hot. I took a bite of shrimp. Okay—this was the right choice."

"She could tell from the picture the scar wasn't there?"

"That's what she thinks, but I think it was decades ago, and men have hairy feet, and the picture wasn't great, so she's imagining things."

"Did you look at the picture yourself?"

Only when I was with Andy, not after. I'd need to do that. I made a face. "Not really. I just thought I'd ask Roxanne, and so I went over there this afternoon, and we were talking, and Rumpole came in." I spooned a hunk of blue crab meat into my mouth and savored it. I'm afraid I hummed. Just a brief little hum. And must have closed my eyes because when I opened them, Lauren was shaking her head. After swallowing, I said, "I can't help it. This is good."

"So what did Roxanne say?"

"That's not really the point. The point I'm trying to make is that Rumpole came in, but Roxanne says she didn't really look at Skip's feet. I guess they weren't into that sort of thing."

"All right now." She looked at me sideways, smirking.

"So this character, who she introduced me to as Jeffrey Downs—more on that in a minute—this guy who is uglier than, to quote a cliché, *homemade soap*—is a real charmer. He opens his mouth, and his voice is like a songbird's would be if it could speak. Delightful. He's smooth and charming. He makes himself at home, sitting down at the table with us." I paused to break some crackers into my gumbo and take a big bite. By this time, I'm afraid it will get cold. Really, the best gumbo I think I've had—at least in a long, long time.

"I never met him when she lived next door to me. I wonder how long they've been together."

After I swallowed, I said, "They say they're best friends. They say they knew each other in high school in California, and by an odd coincidence, both had moved to Galveston. When they flew out to California to a class reunion, they met again and found out they both lived here."

"Humph. So are they romantically involved? Lovers?"

"Well, I wouldn't be if I were her. She's pretty good looking, and he's—he's—well I wouldn't want to see him out from under the sheets even in the dim light."

Lauren scraped the bottom of her bowl and put the last of her gumbo in her mouth, pushing her bowl away. She pulled her mug toward her. "I'm kind of getting confused here. What exactly is your point in all this?"

I patted my stomach. I was getting full, but the gumbo was so good. I probably shouldn't have had three beers. "I happen to know he's married to someone else."

Her eyes flared. "No kidding. How do you know that if you've just met him?"

"Do you know Etta? She's an artist. She lives just down the street—across from the art gallery next door to Mod Coffeehouse."

"Have I met her?" She glanced toward the restaurant entrance and shook her head. "I don't think so. When would I have? Oh, you mean not with you. Have I met her since I moved to Galveston?" She shook her head. "Not unless at an Artwalk, maybe I've seen her work, or just in passing. I don't get down here that much."

"I was at her condo the other day. She was showing me around, and we were on the roof when this yellow Beamer raced up, and a man got out, and she said he was her husband."

"I think it's Bimmer. Rhymes with shimmer."

"What?"

"BMW cars are called Bimmers."

"I thought that's what I said, Bimmer."

She shook her head. "Sounded like you said Beamer. It's Bimmer. Look it up."

"Whatever," I said, "anyway, since I'd seen this *Bimmer* outside Roxanne's house I told Etta I had to go, and I ran out of there. I lucked out that he went into Mod before coming to the condo, so he didn't see me."

"Where is all this leading to?"

I pushed my bowl aside and took a long drink of water. I was through with beer for the night, early though it still was. "I didn't want to meet him because Etta had already confided in me that she wasn't happy and was considering her options for the future."

"You just met her? That was quick."

"She's really nice. I met her kind of by accident at Mod when I was talking to this older man who turned out to be her neighbor and friend, so when she came to get coffee, he introduced us. When she heard I was looking at condos, thinking I might want to buy one, she said she was thinking of selling, and did I want to come see hers? So I did."

"Whew." She shook her head. "I didn't know you were contemplating buying a condo here."

"Dreaming about it is more like it."

"I'm confused. Was there a reason why you wanted to see those condos?"

"Just curiosity because I'd followed Rumpole from Roxanne's one day and saw him go inside that building. I just thought it wouldn't hurt to get a look at one of them."

"Uh-huh."

"Well, I didn't have anything else to do that day."

She laughed again. "Sure. Which day was that?"

I grinned. "But what I'm wondering now is whether I should tell Etta that Jeffrey is Roxanne's *best friend.*"

Her eyes widened, and her eyebrows drew together. "Why would you want to do that? It doesn't have anything to do with the murder investigation you're working on for Isley."

"She's just so nice. She doesn't deserve that. Anyway, it could help her make her mind up about what she wants to do."

"You know, Mavis, we've only been friends for a few days too, but I have to tell you this. That's none of your business."

I didn't quite feel like I'd been gut punched, but I was taken aback. I stared at her for a few minutes and drank some more water.

"Will there be anything else, ladies?" It was the waiter.

"Just the check," Lauren said. "Separate checks."

"You're right," I said to her. "I don't even really know this lady. I just went over to her condo to see what they looked like, and she started telling me stuff—well, actually before we even got there. I just feel like I have a responsibility to her."

"For what? Don't you think your time would be better spent trying to figure out this murder?"

"I'm tempted to call up Isley and tell her what everyone's said about her brother and see if I can get her to give up. From all reports, he was a real—a real, I don't know, mad man, sociopath? Split-personality? Narcissist? I'm no psychologist or social worker, but I took a few courses in college. He sure as heck wasn't normal." The waiter returned with our checks. We got out our credit cards and scooted through the aisle between the tables to the front to pay.

"I hope you're not angry with me," Lauren said. "Want to go over to Mod and get some coffee or tea? Or Hey Mikey's for ice cream?"

"I'd better stick with coffee or tea. I already had enough calories this evening, thanks." We crossed the street and walked down to Mod. After we received our orders, we grabbed a table at the far corner of the room in the area that's more of a lounge. "I could live in Galveston very easily." I sipped my coffee. I'm not a coffee freak and used to hate it, but I'm liking it better all the time, even without all that goopy stuff. Coffee can be bitter, but sometimes bitter is good.

"So what are you going to do tomorrow?" Lauren stretched out her legs and leaned back. "Do you have other people to talk to? Didn't those weird people in the scary house give you the name of someone else to see?"

"Yeah, but he's incarcerated. That doesn't mean I can't see him, I just have to do some planning."

"Mavis?"

I heard a familiar voice. When I turned around, Etta was standing behind me. She looked pretty much like she had the last time I'd seen her, long skirt and all, but tired-looking. She held a paper cup of something.

"I thought that was you." She smiled. "Who's your friend? May I join you?"

Lauren and I exchanged looks. "Sure. Let me switch chairs, and you can sit here. This is Lauren, by the way. She used to be a court reporter in Houston. Lauren, Etta."

After we got settled, Etta said, "What have you been up to? Working on something important?"

"Always. You been up to anything good?"

Etta sighed dramatically. See, even if I wanted to stay out of

169

someone's business, what am I supposed to do when they invite me in? "What's the matter? You seem a little down."

She glanced from my face to Lauren's. "I don't want to bother you girls."

If that wasn't an invitation… "It's okay. If Lauren hasn't heard just about everything in the world as a court reporter then I'm, well, whatever." That was all it took. Etta opened her mouth, and her story poured out.

She swallowed from her drink and set it on the table. "My marriage is what's wrong. I told you I was thinking of selling my condo. Well, I'm pretty sure I am. I haven't been happy for a long time. Jeffrey," she looked at Lauren, "that's my husband, has been so indifferent to me—not only sexually, but every other way. He doesn't touch me at all except a peck on the cheek when he's about to leave town. He mostly ignores me when he's home. He's always on his computer looking at whatever he's into—stuff he doesn't need—and he's gone more now than he ever has been."

I knew why, but my eyes met Lauren's, and I didn't say anything. As Etta talked, I wondered if she'd been drinking or had taken drugs because she really was letting it all hang out. Not that her words were slurred or anything like that.

Etta said, "I hate to even think about a divorce. I still love him. I believe in keeping commitments, and I made a commitment twenty years ago that I thought would be forever and ever." A tear rolled down her cheek. She sniffed and blew her nose into her napkin.

I sipped my coffee and studied her. Lauren did the same. Neither of us said anything.

"I've never been married before, but he was married to a shrew who'd made his life miserable. At least that's what he said. Now I wonder… Anyway, he said I was so different that he knew we'd be happy for the rest of our lives. He grew up poor, worked his way through college, got his degree, and was making a good living, when his wife bankrupted him and left him. I promised I'd never leave." She took another sip and looked at me over her cup. "We've had a good life, we have nice things—cars, condo, and all. We traveled a lot, all over the world, but I don't think he loves me anymore. I'm starting to wonder if he ever loved me." She broke down and sobbed into her hands. She raised her head and took the napkins Lauren retrieved from the table next to us. She pressed them against her face for a few moments. I gestured to Lauren, palms up like what am I supposed to do?

Etta cleared her throat. "You think I'm a silly old woman, I know. I just can't decide what to do." She looked from one to the other of us. "I think he married me for my money. Remember I told you, Mavis, that the condo is mine? I don't know if I said I'm a trust baby."

I'd known that about her anyway. Ian had told me the morning I'd sat next to him here. Before I met her.

Etta cried a bit more and then said, "It's just so unreal. I feel like you feel when someone dies, you know? You wake up and then remember they died, and it hurts all over again. Could I have been that gullible? For twenty years?" Her face wore a stricken look, deep lines expressed themselves from the inside out. "Could he really have married me for my money, and I didn't know it? We have a large insurance policy on me that's very costly—our financial planner talked us into a million-dollar policy. We have a smaller one on him." Her face grew grim. "I go from sad to a state of disbelief to anger when I think of him fooling me, lying to me all this time, and I didn't see it. He puts on that charming act, uses that charming voice, cajoles me and anyone else who's around. I've been thinking of cancelling that insurance policy, Mavis, because now I don't trust him. What do you think?" Her eyes searched mine. "I could cancel it, sell the condo secretly, move away, and file for divorce." She broke into tears again and continued to cry softly as Lauren and I just sat there. She muttered, "He's gone so much, he might not even notice."

After a little while, I asked, "Where's your neighbor Ian, Etta? I'm thinking maybe he could come over here and walk you home."

"I'm sorry I burdened you with this. Let me call him on my cell." She pulled a phone out of her pocket and pressed a button. After a moment, she said into the phone, "Could you come to Mod and take me home? I'm not feeling very well."

"You didn't burden us, Etta." I tried to act cheerful. "We're women, and we need to stick together."

She nodded and sighed. "I'm just so tired." She looked hard into my eyes. "I don't know why I like you so much—why I trust you since I just met you, but I do."

"I appreciate that." I took her hand. "If you want, after you get some rest, I'll come back. How about tomorrow morning? We could talk some more. Would you like that?"

"I imagine I'm acting like a doddering old woman, aren't I? But I'm really not that old." She stood. "My parents, now they're old. In their nineties. Remember I told you they're in Kerrville? Maybe I'll at least go pay them a visit."

"I think that's a good idea. Don't you, Lauren?"

Lauren, whose face wore a frown, who hadn't spoken or done anything but get the napkins for Etta to wipe her face, said, "Sounds like it to me. It would give you some time to think about things. To clear your head."

Ian walked up, looking like the sweetest thing, concern written all over him. "I'm glad you called me, sweetie," he said. "Let's get you home."

Lauren and I watched as Ian led Etta back through Mod. What an ending to an interesting day.

Chapter 18

SLEPT IN AGAIN ON WEDNESDAY. BY that, I mean I didn't get up until around eight. When I had office days in Houston, I'd often get up and go for a run, but summertime in Galveston? I may be nuts, but I'm not stupid. I don't want to clean out my pores that bad. The condo facility had a tiny place they referred to as a gym. After I'd had what purported to be breakfast: coffee and a can of vegetable juice, I sashayed down there, and since the only other piece of equipment—a treadmill—was occupied, rode a stationary bicycle for an hour in the air conditioning.

Before we parted the night before, Lauren and I agreed she would head over to Roxanne's early in the morning to see whether Rumpole made an appearance. I would go see Etta at Mod since I'd promised to do so. If Lauren had something to report, she'd call or come down to the shop. She was really liking the detective business. I hoped she wasn't going to want part of my fee.

If what Etta's friend, Ian, had said the other day was true, Etta didn't arrive at Mod Coffee House until around ten. I had plenty of time to shower and get downtown and casually run into Etta, which wouldn't be a big thing, since she'd kind of invited me to visit with her again. Besides, I knew Mod had some mouth-watering goodies I could brunch on.

When I arrived back at my condo unit, I was about to unlock my door when someone rushed up to me, causing a flare of adrenaline to spurt through my body. Jumping back, I dropped my keys. Tim, Chuck's partner, stood there smiling. "What the hell?" I yelled. And wished I'd had my gun, but as usual, it was locked in my glovebox. Not that I'd have shot Tim, but he could have been anybody.

"Did I startle you?" In addition to his sweet smile, Tim wore sunglasses with tropical flower frames and red lenses. Normal Galveston beachwear? I may have spent the better part of a week there, but I still didn't have an idea about how Islanders customarily dress. I recognized him by his build and walking shorts and sleeveless designer T-shirt. "I didn't mean to." His fresh woodsy aftershave surrounded him like an aura.

"Back up," I said. "How'd you even know where I'm staying?" I didn't like the idea that I was easy to track down. I couldn't see his eyes, so I had to put my faith in his words and body language. His stance wasn't threatening, and he followed my order, taking a couple of steps back until he was out of my personal space.

He shrugged one shoulder. "I followed you?"

"Is that a question?"

"Okay. I followed you—for sure." His disarming demeanor made him appear nonthreatening.

Not really wanting to know when, I crouched down to get my keys while keeping my eyes on him. He could easily overpower me. After all, I'm just a defenseless woman, right? "You followed me because…"

"Chuck is so upset. I wanted to keep tabs on how your investigation is going."

He sounded sincere enough, but was his following me more than that? "You couldn't call?"

"Um…I did try to call you last night, but you never picked up."

I punched the passcode into my phone, concealing the keyboard from Tim, of course, and checked my voice mail. "No voice mails." I'd already cleared Ben's when I was on the bike. We'd had a sweet conversation. But that's beside the point.

"I didn't leave one. But I called you at least three times. Look at your recents."

"Whatever, but exactly what is it you want to know?" I could check my calls later. I had become conscious of my own attire, leggings and a holey T-shirt from a women's march a decade earlier, and my body odor from working up a sweat while on the stationary bike. My hair was a mess, too. What was wrong with me? Who cared? He was gay, and I was in a relationship. So anyway, why was he there? Did he have ill intentions. I didn't think so, but someone famous once said, "Suspect everyone," which I apparently needed to heed. "And what is it you want to know so badly you'd stalk me?"

"I wouldn't look at it like that, Mavis."

"Okay. So just tell me. I've got a life I need to get to."

"Uh…well, do you think Chuck killed his father?" He removed his glasses, revealing bloodshot eyes. His forehead was wrinkled and drawn together.

I had no idea what was in his brain but wondered whether he could be frightened for Chuck. Or of Chuck.

"Has Chuck ever been violent with you?"

"No, but…uh…no one knows what someone will do when they're really angry. And Chuck can get really angry."

"Let me get this straight. You're afraid of Chuck?"

"Could we go inside? It's really hot and sticky out here."

"No." I held my hand like a stop-sign. "What happened? Did y'all have a fight? Did he threaten you?"

"I think the stress of the investigation is getting to him."

"But he drinks. That's how he handles it. He drinks, you said. What's changed?"

"You showed up. Since the other day, he's been different. I guess you could say an angry drunk as opposed to a sloppy, passed out drunk." He was moving about on the balls of his feet. Did he need to use the facilities, or was he just antsy? "And so I was wondering, do you know when you might finish up? And also, would you advise me to maybe take a trip—get away from Chuck for a while?"

I searched his face. Was that all? I mean, was he after something else? Maybe wondering whether I considered him a suspect? Which I hadn't until he showed up. He didn't have a motive as far as I could see, except to avenge Chuck for the way his father had treated him. Was that motive enough? I don't know. Timmy really didn't seem the type to ax someone to death. If there was a type.

I took him by the arm and walked him down the balcony to where the elevator was and pushed the button. "Tell you what, why don't you go someplace for a few days. Do you have a mother you could visit? Or a sibling?"

"Yeah, in Dallas. I could go see my little nieces and nephews for a few days."

I wouldn't wish Dallas on anyone during the summer, but if it would make Tim feel better… "So do that. Give Chuck some excuse about missing your little relatives." I gave him the side-eye. "Just be sure you come back."

"But who will bring him home from the bars? Who will take care of him?"

He was beginning to get on my last nerve. "Okay, don't go visit your little nieces and nephews then. Stay here. What do you want from me? I'm not going to go get him out of the bars."

"You don't have to be so grouchy. Could you just tell me if you think he did it, that's all?"

I resisted the temptation to roll my eyes. "I have no idea." And if I knew, I wouldn't tell him. I really didn't have any idea why he had come to me. Did Chuck send him? Or was he really frightened of Chuck? Was he wondering whether I thought one of them was a suspect? If so, which one? Or was it just to let me know he knew where I lived—at least temporarily—in some kind of implied threat? "Tell you what, though, if I conclude that Chuck murdered his father, you'll be one of the first people I tell. In the meantime, you have to decide whether you want to stay with him while I try to solve this case, or whether you'll feel safer elsewhere."

When the elevator door opened, I pushed him in. "Goodbye. And Tim, leave a message next time. I have a gun, and if I get startled, I could shoot someone by accident." I showed him some teeth as the door closed on his somewhat astonished-looking face.

As soon as I knew Tim was long gone, I ran downstairs to my car and retrieved my gun from the locked glovebox. When I got back in my room, I tucked it into my purse. If Tim could find me, others could too. Not that I thought anyone was out to get me, but….

Chapter 19

WHEN I ARRIVED AT MOD COFFEE House a little later on Wednesday morning, Etta wasn't there, but Lauren was. Again, she wore white, but this time, a white cotton sundress, white sandals, and white sunglasses which adorned the top of her head. Me, I was dressed in formal wear: a pair of cargo pants and a green T-shirt under a long-sleeved plaid cotton shirt that posed as a jacket. While I hadn't seen Lauren's outfit before, she'd seen everything I'd brought with me, all of which was getting pretty ripe. I told myself I was wearing Island Casual.

Lauren sat at the exact same table we'd sat at the night before, but in the corner chair, facing out, where she could see everything. I didn't know why she was helping me so much, boredom on her part, I think. When everything was over, I'd have to find a way to thank her. "Have you been here a while?" When I dropped my purse on the table, it landed with a clunk, reminding me of what was inside.

"Not long. When Rumpole left, I came straight over." She wiggled her eyebrows at me and smiled like she was having the time of her life.

"When he left..." That sounded promising. "Let me get my coffee and something to eat. The smell of some kind of bread baking is making my stomach rumble. I'll be right back." Because of the gun inside, I took my purse with me to the other room while I placed my order.

I didn't want to spend a lot of time at Mod, just enough to keep my promise to Etta and to eat something yummy. I hoped to see Ben later, to ask him to go over what I knew about the case. I was learning to ask for help—especially from someone who wasn't involved. Maybe he'd have a different perspective.

I also wanted Margaret to look into where Axel Waterman was in the prison system. Since she was so good on the computer, I figured she could track him down and find out what was involved in my meeting with him at whatever prison in which he was housed. I might as well get it over with, see what he had to say. If Captain Linden had been actively engaged in illicit activities at the time of his death, maybe Waterman could point me in the right direction. Doubtful, but it could happen.

After I picked up my order, I slid into a chair across from Lauren and kept my purse in my lap. "So, tell." I slurped my coffee before taking a big bite of zucchini bread.

Lauren pushed her coffee cup forward and leaned over it, covering half her mouth with her hand. She smelled like rosemary, which I knew Roxanne used as a hedge around her house. "I arrived there at six and parked down the street. I didn't think Roxanne would recognize my car, but she could."

"Six A.M.?" I almost swallowed my tongue. The woman really was dedicated.

"I wanted to be sure and see him if he arrived early this morning. You know, he could have left the house early, told Etta he was going to exercise or something."

"I could be wrong, but I think Etta said he was out of town." My stomach stopped making audible gurgling sounds, showing appreciation for solid food.

She nodded. "Anyway, his car wasn't there when I arrived, so I waited a couple of hours."

"You didn't, by chance, go peek in Roxanne's windows?"

Her lips tightened over her teeth, and her eyes grew wide. "What made you think that?"

"You're practically wearing a rosemary bush. I guess you can't smell yourself."

She glanced down at her dress and back up at me. "Oh, you don't mean literally."

I nodded and watched her face as she looked surprised and grinned. "Okay, well after a while, several hours I guess, I drove around to the back of Roxanne's house when I didn't see any action out front. I counted the number of houses from the corner and figured out which one was hers. There were bushes on each side of the garage door."

"And…"

"Well…I did get out and look through the little glass windows into her garage."

I shook my head. "You are one crazy broad."

She grabbed my hand as I was getting ready to fork another bite of that delicious zucchini bread into my mouth. "Mavis, was I surprised when I saw his car in her garage!"

My stomach clenched. "You do realize you could get into trouble for that. Like arrested as a peeping Tom."

She sat up straight. "Of course I do." She hunkered down again. "But I left quickly and drove back out to the front where I parked catty-corner from her house." She shivered. "I was even more surprised when about five minutes later, I saw that ugly car pull out of the alley."

I flinched. "No way. You really could have been caught."

"It was so exciting though." Her eyes sparkled. She leaned back and sipped from a glass of some kind of pink juice. "No wonder you do this for a living."

Ignoring that, I said, "Did you follow him?"

"No. I guess I should have, but I came straight here. He turned left, heading north, away from me."

"Obviously he parks in her garage when he's spending the night. Best friends, my ass." Did Roxanne really think they were fooling anyone?

"If they're best friends, they're best friends with benefits." Lauren laughed.

"Poor Etta. Now we know for sure. Should we tell her?"

"Shh. Here she comes," Lauren said.

I turned in my chair and watched the little woman as she inched her way around the other chairs and tables until she arrived at ours. She dressed just as artsy as before, in another long flowery skirt, a tank top, and sandals. I wondered whether she had anything else in her wardrobe.

"Good morning, ladies." A wan smile crossed her face. "It's nice to see you back down here."

"I promised you I'd come back this morning," I said. "Did you sleep well?"

"Hardly a wink," she said. "I'll return after I get my drink." She put her keys on the table.

When Etta was out of earshot, Lauren said, "You know, Mavis, I've been thinking about it. I took down a lot of testimony in a lot of different kinds of cases over the years, and I think I know what's up with her husband."

"Yeah, he's committing adultery, the jerk."

"Besides that. Etta said he's indifferent to her. She described his coming and going and spending hours on his computer and buying that stupid-looking car and that she thinks he married her for her money. I think he's a sociopath."

"That's your professional opinion?" I could have bitten my tongue. Lauren was helping, and I needed to be nicer.

She scrunched her nose at me. "You can be sarcastic if you want, but we had more than one case like that."

"He's never hit her or abused her in any way—at least she didn't give any indication of that."

"Not all sociopaths are dangerous. They have big egos and like to feel important and like excitement. I heard of this woman once who was a Miss Something or other, like the name of a city. She was a model when she met her husband, and he'd introduce her to people and tell them she was a model and that she had been Miss Whatever-it-was." She pointed her finger at me. "She testified that it took her a long time to figure him out."

"I don't think Etta was a trophy wife. She's an artist. Not even particularly famous from what I gather."

"Yes, but she has money. He very well could've married her for her money. She said they travel, or traveled, a lot. That would be exciting to a sociopath. In the case I was telling you about, the man wanted the woman to continue modeling long after they were married. They didn't need the money." Lauren watched over my shoulder. "She wanted to have children. She got pregnant, and he made her get an abortion. He didn't want kids, didn't want to take care of a kid. He didn't even want a dog."

I thought about what she said. He married a woman older than himself. She had big bucks. His being a sociopath would answer a lot of questions. Whether he could be, or had ever been violent, remained to be seen. "Etta and Rumpole have no kids."

"Do they have a pet?"

"I didn't see any signs of one when I was in the condo." I tried to recall if I'd seen any evidence of any kind of pet. I didn't. Not even a bird or a hamster.

"And didn't you tell me he was charming—that he had a voice like a TV personality's? Shh. Here she comes. We can discuss it more later."

I glanced over my shoulder. Etta carried an over-sized cup and saucer with both hands, as if she didn't trust herself not to drop them. I pulled out the chair between myself and Lauren. "Need help?"

She sighed. "I'm not very steady this morning. I think I've made a decision." Her hands shook as she set the cup on the table and slid into the chair. Glancing from me to Lauren, she said, "I'm going to leave him. I'm going to move to Kerrville."

"Wow," Lauren said. "That's where your parents are, right?"

"Yes." She sipped from her cup. "I'll go see them this weekend, and while I'm there, I'll look around for a house to buy."

"Sounds like that might be the best thing for you," I said. If she was going to go ahead and divorce him, there was no reason for us to tell her what he was up to.

"I haven't been happy for a long time. I've been thinking about this for a couple of years—can't remember exactly when. I think it was about two years ago that he really became indifferent to me. Could have been earlier, and I just didn't notice." She took another sip and put her napkin to her lips.

I couldn't remember when Roxanne said she and Rumpole met at the class reunion or whether she even said. Could it have been two years ago?

Etta wrapped her hands around her cup as if to warm them. "Mmm. I do like their coffee here, but I suppose there are good coffee places in the Hill Country. And other artists, too. In fact, I know there are because I've been to some art exhibits up there."

"Up where?" a deep, melodious male voice asked from behind me.

The hair rose on the back of my neck. Lauren's eyes grew wide and round. I glanced up over my shoulder, and there stood Rumpole in well-pressed tan slacks, a short-sleeved dress shirt, brown leather loafers, and about two days growth of beard. I couldn't be sure, but he might have grown another chin since I first met him, hidden under those whiskers. When our eyes made contact, he grimaced and the muscle in his jaw flexed. I could just imagine what was going through his head. Something like *Holy shit*, I'll bet.

Etta put down her cup and stuck out her chin. "Kerrville. Where my parents live." She looked from him to me and then Lauren. "Lauren, Mavis, this is my husband, Jeffrey. Jeffrey, these are some new friends of mine, Mavis and Lauren."

Lauren avoided my eyes when she put out her hand to shake his. "Nice to meet you."

He shook her hand and, dropping it, looked at me. I stuck my hand out, too, and said, "You look awfully familiar. Have we met before?" He almost broke my metacarpals with his grip. The look in his eye was similar to his handshake—as though he'd like to break the bones in my neck.

"No, I don't think so," he said, finally letting go of my hand, which I was sure would at least be bruised. "I would have remembered a beautiful redhead like you." His tone couldn't have been more charming.

"I thought you were out of town," Etta said. "I wasn't expecting you until Friday late."

The three of us were all turned in his direction, craning to look up at him.

He said, "Seems the last couple of my customers were headed to some kind of convention, so I came home."

My neck was beginning to hurt. Was Etta going to ask him to join us? Not wanting to get into the middle of a conversation between husband and wife, I stood too. "Hey, I'll leave y'all to have your coffee. I need to get to my office."

"I've gotta go too," Lauren said. She glanced at her watch. "I'm about to be late for a dental appointment."

I could swear Etta's eyes were pleading for us to stay, but she was going to have to be a big girl and break the news to him by herself, if that's what she intended to do. I patted her arm. "I'll see you later, Etta." I wrapped the remainder of my zucchini bread in a napkin and put it in my purse.

Lauren merely said her goodbyes and joined me in my quick trip toward the door. As we departed, Etta said to him, "I'm going to visit my parents this weekend. It's been a while."

We didn't wait to hear his response.

"They sure don't look compatible," Lauren said when we were a good distance away. "But I've seen that before. When I took down testimony in child support hearings, I had a hard time imagining some of the couples together, like *What was she thinking when she had sexual relations with that—*"

"I get your drift. He probably charmed the pants off her with that voice of his."

Lauren laughed.

I elbowed her as we marched down the sidewalk toward my car. I laughed too. "I'm worried about her. Do you think she looked afraid of him?"

"I couldn't say. When she was looking at him, her back was to me." She pulled her keys out of her purse. "This is me." We stopped at her car. "He could really hurt her if he tried. He's so much larger than she is, taller, and did you see his arms? He has some muscles there."

"Yeah, but he's never hit her. You're the one who said not all sociopaths hurt people."

"At least physically." Lauren pressed on her key fob, unlocking the car.

"Did you see her shy away from him? I think he at least browbeats her. Well, I'll let you go, so you can make your appointment."

"There's no appointment." She opened her door. A rush of hot air enveloped both of us. We stepped back farther on the sidewalk. She clicked another button on her key fob, and her car started. "What are you going to do now?"

I sniffed at my underarms. "I was thinking I'd drive to Houston, go by my house and get some more clothes, then head over to my office. I need to talk to my staff and see if anything's going on and see Ben."

She nodded. "Uh-huh. But you've decided against that?"

"I'm getting awfully sick of driving up and down Interstate 45. I think I'll go back to the condo and do some laundry. While my clothes are washing, I could call the office and maybe catch Ben as well."

"You can use my washer and dryer if you want." Lauren put one foot inside her car.

"Nah, but thanks. I need to spread out my notes and review them with Ben and see if he has any ideas about what direction to go next. When I spoke to him this morning, he agreed to let me run some things past him."

"I get it," she said. "I really shouldn't be privy to all that information. Mavis, are you thinking Rumpole had anything to do with Captain Linden's murder?" She held onto the door, which separated the two of us.

"I don't know. I need to find out when that class reunion was, that's for sure." Now, that would be too easy, if Rumpole had committed the murder. But the police surely would have figured that out a long time ago. Wouldn't they? "Maybe we can talk later? When's your husband coming back?"

"Tomorrow night, probably. Maybe as late as Friday afternoon." She climbed inside. "Keep me posted, will you?"

I nodded and waved and turned toward my car. I glanced back at Mod. Rumpole stood watching me through the high glassed wall. We made eye contact for only a moment. I shivered but didn't increase my pace. I didn't want him to think I could be intimidated.

Chapter 20

BEFORE I WENT TO DO MY laundry, I drove back to the place that had made the checkerboard copy of Isley's brother's body and ran in with the photograph. Asking nicely, I persuaded them to give me a free do-over, including sending the photo to my phone so I could proof it. This time, there were no checkerboard patterns, so I had them send it to Isley. The young woman behind the counter looked at me oddly. Was it because I'd sent a photo of a dead body or because my clothes emitted an odor? Didn't matter. I could at least take care of the latter when I returned to the condo.

As soon as I arrived, I changed into my workout clothes, which were possibly more offensive-smelling than my other clothes, but I was unlikely to come across anyone while wearing them. No one was around. No one else doing laundry. No one walking around the complex that I could see. Few cars in the parking lot. Most tourists were probably at the beach or on The Strand, shopping. After starting the washer down in the laundry room, I returned to the condo and called my office.

Margaret answered. "Mavis, why're you calling? I thought you were coming up here today."

Pulling the phone a good distance from my ear, I said, "Change of plans." Margaret could get quite loud on a phone.

"Well, I'm glad to hear from you. I've missed you so much."

What was that about? "It's only been a few days since we've seen each other. Is something wrong? Are you okay? Is Candy okay? Did either of you burn the place down?"

"Everything's fine. I just miss you. When you're gone, it seems like forever. I wish I could go down there and help you. How's the case going?"

So that was it. What she really wanted was to be involved in the Linden case. "I have some ideas about what could have happened, but nothing solid. So things are okay?"

"Candy's out serving papers again. She's gotten really good at it, and she likes it too. She thinks it's funny when she sees the surprise on their faces at someone like her handing them court service."

"Someone like her—she's still wearing her school uniform?" I found that extremely amusing. Maybe as she grew older, we could get her a Girl Scout leader's outfit.

"Yep. She thinks it's especially funny because school has been out for the summer for weeks, and apparently, the people she serves with court papers don't even think about that."

"She's a good girl. I just hope she's being careful. Don't forget about my run-in with that dog last week." I touched the place on my face where he'd clawed me.

"She's very careful. She claims she can run faster than you."

That was probably true. "Tell her we're not in competition."

"Okay." In a quieter voice, Margaret said, "Is that woman still helping you down there? That court reporter?"

Margaret, if not jealous, was at least worried she was being replaced.

"She has some free time on her hands right now, that's all. So what else is going on? Anything in the mail?"

"A lot of junk. A few small checks. Oh, and a lawyer called, wanting you to do some divorce work for him. I told him you're out of town but made an appointment for his client next week."

"That's cool. Any idea what he had in mind?"

"It's really a child support case. They've been divorced a couple of years. The lawyer wants you to follow the ex-husband and see where he goes and where he's working. He says the guy claims he's unemployed and can't pay child support."

"That sounds nice and uncomplicated. I like cases that come from lawyers. They always pay us."

"And there was a walk-in. I made him an appointment too. He wouldn't tell me what he wanted. He was an old man, like in his sixties or thereabouts, but said he'd definitely be back."

"Good job, Margaret. I'm surprised the lawyer would tell you anything."

"You know, Mavis, if I wasn't stuck in this office, I could do something like that. Follow that ex-husband."

I thought about that for a moment. Could Margaret handle that and let Candy watch the front desk? Or maybe they could alternate? "I'll think about it. In the meantime, I have something I want you to do."

"Anything. You know I want to help, but I'm stuck in the office."

"I heard you the first time. I need you there. Or somebody there. We'll talk when I get back."

"What is it you want me to do?"

"Ah, what you do best. Research. You think you could track down the high school a couple of people went to in California and find out when their class reunion was?"

"If you give me their names, sure. Might take me awhile, but that shouldn't be too hard."

"Okay." I almost said Rumpole of the Bailey. "Jeffrey Downs and Roxanne Linden, though that's not her maiden name. She would have had a different name in high school."

"Who are they?"

"That's Isley's brother's widow and current friend."

"Like boyfriend?"

"If you can call someone in the fourth or fifth decade of his life a boyfriend, then yeah. I just realized I don't know how old either of them is."

"I think in their fifties or sixties, at least, judging by Isley. So I guess I'll start with that assumption. And I'll start with him. If I can find him, I can find her. And I know what you're going to say about assuming something, so don't even go there."

"I also need you to track down one Axel Waterman, who I think may be in the federal prison system, but if not, try TDCJ."

Someone knocked on the condo door. I hoped it wasn't Tim again. "Listen, gotta go. I'll call you later." I clicked off and left my phone on the dinette table next to my purse. I wasn't in the mood to baby Tim. Ready to be firm with him, to tell him to bug off, I jerked the condo door open.

"Mavis Davis," Rumpole said in a tone that was anything but friendly. Gone was the charm he'd turned on both times I'd met him. "I need to talk to you." His forefinger pointed to my chest as if it were a .45 about to go off. He wasn't much taller than I, but he was a man. They have different muscle sets from us. Even if I worked out with weights regularly—well, at all—he would still have the advantage.

Adrenalin coursed through every vein and artery in my body. I glanced over at my purse, fixing in my mind just how far it was from my reach. "What are you doing here, Mr. Downs?" I didn't invite him in.

"Do you know how upset you've made my wife?" He put one hand on one side of the doorframe and the other on the other and leaned toward me, blocking any possible exit.

I backed up a step. "Me? All I did was lend her an ear."

"Did you tell her about me and Roxanne?" His voice had held a menacing tone since he first opened his mouth, and it wasn't getting any better.

"I thought y'all were just friends."

"So you did tell her?" His eyes became slits.

"I most certainly did not. I'd never do such a thing." I'd never admit to it, anyway.

"You probably don't know this, but Etta suffers from severe depression."

I could understand why, but I wasn't going to say that right then either. I nodded. "She didn't tell me that."

"She doesn't usually share that with people. Would you? I think she's gone off her medication. I'm really worried about her. She's acting strange." His shoulders slumped like he was downcast, but I figured it was an act.

"Ru—Jeffrey, I don't know her well. I just met her the other day at Mod, but she seems okay. Why don't you suggest she see a doctor or take her to one, if you're concerned about her?"

His eyes darted over my shoulder. "I'm going to do that. I'm going to do that next week." His eyes didn't meet mine. "I have to watch her very closely until then. She could harm herself before I can get her to a doctor."

She didn't seem like she had any inclination to do that. Get away from him, yes. Go for a visit to Kerrville, yes. But hurt herself? I don't think so. "So what do you want from me? Why'd you come here?"

He stood up to his full height and took a step forward, across the threshold. "To tell you not to go around her anymore."

I stepped closer to my purse. I didn't like to be told what to do. I especially didn't like to be told what to do by overbearing men. A burning sensation had begun in my gut. "My having coffee with her has nothing to do with you." Okay, so it didn't start having anything to do with him…okay, well I guess it did, since I wanted to see inside the building. So the situation had evolved. Now it really had something to do with him.

"I said, you gotta quit going down there. Quit talking to my wife, or—"

"Or what? Are you threatening me?"

"If you want to take it that way. I'm just warning you. Leave her alone."

I couldn't leave *it* alone. "And if I don't. If I go for a cup of coffee at Mod, and I see her? Then what?"

The muscles in his jaws flexed. His nostrils flared. His face grew pink. He drew in a deep breath. I took a step closer to my shoulder bag. I didn't want him to see how scary I thought he was. I didn't want him to realize what I was doing.

"Just stay away from there. There's lots of other coffee shops in Galveston. No reason for you to go all the way downtown." His face had gone from pink to red. His voice held none of the melodious notes he'd put on the night before or that day at Roxanne's.

I had the sensation of being in a drawdown situation, like on *Gunsmoke*, though neither of us had a gun in our hand. I hoped to remedy that momentarily. "Look, Mr. Downs—"

"No! You look." He took another step forward and was completely inside the condo. I wondered whether he'd been looking over my shoulder to see if anyone else was there. "Just stay away from my wife!"

I reached my purse just as he gave that last order. I slipped my hand inside and pulled out the zucchini bread. He took a couple of strides toward me, reaching me just as I managed to come up with my .38 the second time I inserted my hand. "Back up right now, Jeffrey Downs."

He stopped, which was a good thing because the table was blocking me from getting further away from him. His face blanched. He raised his hands. It was a good thing he had the presence of mind to respond to the appearance of a gun. I generally don't believe in violence, but since

I've been in this business, I've been a victim too many times. If he'd kept on coming, I would have shot him. I have no doubt about that.

"Get the hell out of here before this thing goes off," I said, my body tense with fear and anger.

He backed up all the way out the door. I followed him. As he turned to leave, he said, "Just remember what I said. Stay away from my wife." He strode down the balcony toward the stairs where he charged down to the parking lot.

I stayed on the balcony myself until I was satisfied he'd driven away, until his yellow BMW was a dot in the distance. Drawing a deep breath, I went back inside for a few moments, putting my revolver on the table next to my purse, to have it ready in case some other fool came calling. I took a moment to steady my hands and to get a drink of water and to assess my situation.

I needed to finish my laundry and get on with my day. I weighed taking my gun with me. Rumpole was gone. I was sure of that, so I risked going downstairs. When I returned to the apartment, I collapsed on the sofa. I needed to breathe easy for a few minutes and think about the whole crazy situation.

Chapter 21

AFTER A FEW MINUTES OF CONTEMPLATION, I phoned my friendly deputy sheriff, Andy Crider. "Hey there, Deputy Crider."

He laughed. "Hey, Mavis Davis. How ya' been, and what do you want?"

"I could just be calling to see how you are."

"Yeah, fat chance. You still with Ben?"

"It's only been a few days, Andy." I restrained myself from giggling. A little flirting never killed anyone.

"You can't blame me for asking. Anyway…"

"Anyway, Andy, I do want something. I want you to run a check on someone."

"You know if it's not a case I'm investigating, I'm not supposed to do that."

"Yeah, I know."

"You know I could get into trouble, be disciplined, etcetera, right?"

"Yeah, I know. But you'll do it, won't you? I hate to ask Ben. Especially when it has to do with the Linden case."

He chuckled again. "I was waiting for you to get to that. Who is it?"

"Well, it seems the Widow Linden has a boyfriend. Personally, I don't find him appealing at all. He's got this *huge* nose, and all his clothes sag on him, making me wonder whether his body sags on him too. I don't know what she sees in him, but apparently, they knew each other in high school. Probably dated back then is my guess."

"So is this a stall?"

Okay, so sometimes I get carried away. "Not at all. His name is Jeffrey—"

"If you say Dahmer—"

"No, I'm being serious. I have to think about his last name. I'm afraid I nicknamed him Rumpole because of his nose."

"Like Rumpole of the Bailey?"

"You know that show too? Downs. His name is Jeffrey Downs, and he's originally from California. I don't know his middle name or much else about him, except he's in his fifties, I think. Oh, and he drives a yellow BMW."

"I've seen that car around Galveston. There can't be more than one like it."

I waited for him to say something else.

Finally, he said, "Are you thinking he killed Captain Linden?"

I took a deep breath. "I…don't…know. I know he and Mrs. Linden hooked up at a class reunion. I don't know when. But over five years ago? I just don't know. But Downs is married. I've met the wife."

"Nice guy. He must be something if two women want him."

"I'm not sure the wife wants him. At least not any more. She's kinda figuring out a way to leave. And I think he's figuring out a way to split from her as well."

"Okay, well, I'll do this for you just this one time on account of as how I'm curious as hell about him too. I'll get back to you a-sap. Take care."

As soon as I clicked off, I received a text from Lauren. "Just wanted to let you know, I drove back by the widow's house after I ran a few errands. Rumpole's car was there, but he left a little while ago. Headed home." I didn't remember her agreeing to shadow him another day. Didn't see any reason to now that we knew he had spent the night with Roxanne. I texted back, "Thanks. He was just here! Talk later."

I called Ben, even though I'd talked to him while riding the bike in the exercise room. I shouldn't bother him during the work day unless it was an emergency. But when had that ever stopped me?

Since my call to Ben was a bust, and my stomach was growling, and there was no food in the refrigerator I'd want to eat, I phoned Etta, who answered on the first ring. "Etta, want to grab some lunch in a little while? I'm doing laundry, but it should be dry soon." Yes, I knew I'd just been warned away from her, but that was beside the point. I wanted to see for myself whether she had any classic signs of depression other than being married to that creep.

"Little late for lunch, Mavis," she said, sounding winded. "I grabbed a sandwich at Mod before I came back here. Just walked in the door."

"That's a long time to stay at a coffee shop. Jeffrey keep you there?" As if I didn't know where he'd been lately.

"Jeffrey left right after you did. Said he was going to make some local calls. I guess that means visit local places where they use his company's drugs or whatever."

An unlikely story if I ever heard one. "Oh, so…"

"Ian came in. He's such a nice man. Hold on while I sit down." There was no sound for a couple of moments. "Okay, well, we talked for such a long time," Etta said.

"Uh huh." Maybe there was something between Ian and Etta. From the outside, they looked like a good match.

"I confided in him. He doesn't want me to leave, but he said he wants what's best for me."

My stomach growled again. I really wanted to finish my laundry and get something to eat. "If Jeffrey left right away, I guess you didn't have any kind of a discussion with him?"

"Just said I was going to visit my parents and probably go on Friday." The phone went silent for a moment again. "I told him I could even go tomorrow night. If he didn't mind." She laughed. "Just being polite to him, Mavis. I've reached the point where I don't care if he minds or not. I've made my decision."

"Okay, then. So, how about dinner?" I still wanted to check her out. She wasn't my responsibility, but I was uneasy with what Rumpole—Jeffrey had said.

"Oh, I'm keeping you from lunch." She'd been reading my mind. "Dinner would be good as long as Jeffrey isn't around. If he is, then I'm telling him. You don't mind, do you?" Her laugh was hollow.

"You sound nervous. Are you going to be okay?"

"Oh, I'm all right." She breathed into the phone. "Thanks for your concern. I'll call you later this afternoon—when I know whether he's going to be here for dinner or not. If you don't hear from me, you call me."

After the call ended, I looked through the peephole. Didn't see anyone. I looked out the window at the parking lot. Empty. I took a chance on running back downstairs for my clothes. They were dry, so I hurried back upstairs, dressed, and drove east on the seawall until I came to a restaurant with a gigantic blue crab on it. They had to have seafood, right?

When I went inside, I took one look at the white tablecloths and made a quick exit. The one next door looked more my style. There, my cargo pants wouldn't stand out. A young Latina gave me a table with a view of the Gulf of Mexico, which was just across Seawall Boulevard. After ordering, I pulled out my phone and scrolled to the little notepad app where I could dictate a few notes.

1. *Captain Linden axed to death 5 years earlier.*
2. *Ax is never recovered.*
3. *Present at the time of the death: Wife. Second son, daughter-in-law, and new baby.*
4. *Wife had concussion from being hit in the head.*
5. *Others uninjured.*
6. *No one saw or heard anything.*
7. *Second son a doper. Now divorced from wife who got custody of child.*
8. *Oldest son, adopted, is alcoholic, not in recovery. Has boyfriend who takes care of him, who is afraid of him.*
9. *Daughter is estranged from just about everyone though some contact with one brother. She's changed her name.*
10. *Decedent may have been involved in shady dealings with scary people. One is in prison.*
11. *Five years later, widow has recovered and sold home and moved to center of town. No visible means of support. She has a married boyfriend (with benefits) who was high school "friend."*
12. *Boyfriend married to trust baby who is unhappy and considering ending relationship.*

My food came, so I put the phone down. I had a lot to think about, which I would do after I ate. Meanwhile, I stared out at the breakers as I consumed my fried shrimp and French fries and tried to calm my mind. The day had been eventful, and it was only half over.

Afterward, I cruised the seawall to the end, driving on what locals called Cherry Hill. People had parked and gotten out, their binoculars pointed at a passing ship. Some waved. In the distance, fishermen bobbed in small boats. Light waves lapped over the rocks between the concrete barrier and the water. I did a U-turn and headed back west. Uneasiness settled over me. Etta was really not my concern, yet I had made her my concern by, okay I admit it, meddling in her affairs. Why was it such a big deal to Rumpole if I had coffee with his wife? Was it because I knew about Roxanne? Or was he trying isolate Etta? Etta lived in a neighborhood of artists and writers and antiquers. No way could he isolate her. I told him I hadn't told Etta about Roxanne. And what if she did find out? That happens often with extra-marital affairs. Was he afraid she'd kick him to the curb? She had all the money.

Roxanne had settled her husband's estate and finally sold the house. She'd bought herself another one. I didn't get the impression she was rolling in the dough, but she was doing okay. At least, she looked like she was doing okay. Rumpole and Etta kept their money separate. He'd had enough to buy himself a BMW. Whether or not he'd paid cash or had car payments, I didn't know, but I could get Margaret to find out. If Etta kicked him out, he'd be left with what? His investments and his car and his personal belongings and whatever dollars he'd squirreled away? Etta would have her trust fund as well as her condo, car, and personal effects. I'd seen the furnishings in her condo. Etta had easily come from money. Big money. I didn't like what I was thinking.

Glancing at my watch, I wondered whether it was too early to call her about dinner. I'd just eaten, but maybe she'd be hungry. I wished Lauren were still watching Jeffrey, so I'd know where he was. I could go by Roxanne's house and check if he was there. Downtown was closer, though.

Downtown won out. Five minutes later, I came to the parking lot for people who live at The Lofts. The yellow Bimmer was there. My stomach became queasy, but I didn't think it was from the shrimp. I pulled over in the alley next to the lot. Grabbing my cell phone, I scrolled to *Recents* and tapped on Etta's number. At the very least, I wanted to tell her I was worried, that I had something to tell her, including I was running a check on her husband. Mostly, I wanted to warn her that her life might be in danger.

"Hey, Mavis," Etta said. "I was just getting ready to call you. Turns out I can't go to dinner with you after all. Jeffrey's home and wants to have a talk. He's in a really good mood, jovial, like his old self, his charming self, the one who convinced me to marry him."

That was not what I wanted to hear. "Could you come down for coffee? Could you meet me at Mod for five minutes? There's something I need to tell you. It's serious."

"Can't. Jeffrey's having a catered meal—shrimp and snapper—delivered here in a few minutes. He took a table and chairs up to the roof a little while ago. He's there now, icing down the Pinot Grigio. I have a feeling he knows how unhappy I've been and wants to make amends."

Holy shit. "Isn't it awfully hot to be having dinner on the roof?"

"He thought of that. He took a big umbrella to put over the table. With the breeze, we should be just fine."

I peeled out of the alley and skirted through the traffic toward her condo. "I'll just be a few minutes, Etta. Please."

"Hold on. He's texting me."

I held my breath. "What's he want?"

"He wants me to come on up and bring the corkscrew."

"Tell him you'll be a few minutes. Just meet me outside, okay?"

"I have to go now. Jeffrey's waiting. I'll call you later, and maybe we can have a drink—or if I'm tied up with Jeffrey…" she snickered. "I'll call you in the morning, and we can do lunch tomorrow."

"Wait, don't hang up!"

The phone went dead

Wending my way around the creeping cars, I headed to Etta's building. One part of my brain said, "Hurry before it's too late." The other said, "I hope you're not crazy as a loon." Didn't matter. I would soon find out.

Chapter 22

I RAN A STOP SIGN AND THEN another and parked alongside the building, next to the fire hydrant. Grabbing my purse, I ran to the glass door. It was locked. I banged and banged. Abigail came moseying out of the elevator. I banged some more.

She unlocked the door. "I remember you. What's going on?"

"I need to get up to Etta's. Etta Downs's condo. She called me and said she needs help." I tried to keep my voice from being too hysterical but still make her understand the urgency. "I think she's had a fall or something. Can you let me up there?" My hands shook.

Abigail studied me for a moment. "I did see you come in with her the other day." She stepped over to the elevator and inserted her key. The door opened right up.

I pushed the button for Etta's floor. As the door closed, I yelled, "Call 911."

Of course, the elevator rose at a sloth's pace. The stairs might have been faster. When the door opened again, I dashed down the hall to Etta's condo. The door was locked. I hammered on it with my fist.

When she didn't answer, I sprinted for the stairs to the roof. I only hoped I was wrong, or if I wasn't wrong, that I wasn't too late.

Taking the stairs two at a time, I fumbled with getting my gun out of my purse. Stairs, stairs, and more stairs. Breathing hard, when I reached the door to the roof, I threw it open.

Rumpole held Etta around her middle, like a rag doll, with her legs dangling down. She struggled and kicked and punched at him. He dragged her toward the edge of the roof, to the thigh-high barrier wall, his face red with exertion.

"Mavis!" Etta screamed, as she tried to free herself.

"Hold it right there, Downs!" I pointed my revolver at him as I ran. He approached the edge. He didn't look like he was going to stop. I yelled, "Move, Etta!" Etta threw her weight away from the edge of the roof. I fired my gun. Jeffrey continued to pull at her. Etta's body was balanced on the barrier wall, the lower part of her torso hanging down, her legs kicking in the air. He was grappling with her arms, trying to grab them and swing her over, while she clawed at the barrier. I fired again. Jeffrey's eyes flared, and he let go of Etta. His arms flailed as he fell over the side.

I dropped my weapon and ran to help Etta, who hung on with both hands, still balancing on her middle. Dropping to my knees, I grabbed her under her arms and pulled. "Hike your leg up if you can." She swung her leg almost over. I managed to pull her toward me until her body fell onto the roof. We both lay there for a few moments, catching our breaths. Finally, I helped her up and wrapped her in my arms as she wept and moaned. I admit to a few tears rolling down my cheeks as well.

I glanced over the side. People were running toward Jeffrey's body. I walked Etta to the table and chairs Jeffrey had set up.

"How did you know?" She mopped her face with the hem of her long skirt. Tears continued streaming down her face.

"Oh, Etta, I've got so much to tell you." I wiped my face on my sleeve.

We comforted each other for a few minutes—intermittently while Etta cried—before being interrupted by the police sirens. I walked back to where he'd gone over. The EMTs were there. A crowd of onlookers had been backed away. Police cars blocked the street in every direction. I picked up my revolver and put it in my purse.

"The police are coming. Do you want the EMTs to look you over?

Her bloodshot eyes met mine. "Not really. I'm sure I'll be sore tomorrow." She blew her nose into one of the napkins from the table. "And have some colorful bruises."

Shaking my head as I spoke, I said, "I can't tell you how sorry I am."

"It's not your fault. How could anyone have known he would do such a thing?" She closed her eyes and clasped her hands in front of her face as if in prayer.

I knew. I would have to tell her what I knew and when but not right then.

A bulky police officer in a dark navy uniform burst through the door to the roof. Before he could say anything, I handed him my purse. "My gun's in there."

"Go sit back down, ma'am." He wore a tag that said Winters.

"Yes, sir." I figured I'd have to go to the police station and answer questions. I wished we could at least get out of the heat. Though we were sitting under the umbrella Jeffrey had so kindly provided, perspiration drenched my body. I glanced at Etta. She was pretty much worse for wear, looking like a wrung-out mop.

The cop had shoved my purse under his arm. I'd have to air it out when I got it back. He took our names and kept his distance as though he thought we might jump him.

"Officer, could we go downstairs to Mrs. Downs's condo? I know you're going to have a lot of questions."

Etta said, "We'd be much more comfortable there."

"I'm waiting for a supervisor," he said. He looked like he thought he should be doing something but didn't know what. "Maybe that would be all right. Let me make a call."

My stomach quivered, along with my hands. I'd never shot anyone before, and now that I was going to have to answer for it, I started wondering what would happen to me. I knew the law in Texas allowed someone to act in defense of another. Would they question whether that was what I'd done? I looked at the officer. "I'm really feeling sick, Officer Winters, like I want to throw up."

He waved me down. He said something about securing the crime scene. What crime was he talking about? I didn't know, and I'm sure he didn't either.

We sat there for another five or so minutes. I got that queasy feeling behind my earlobes that indicated throwing up was imminent. I turned away from Etta and the cop and heaved. After a second heave-ho, Etta handed me some paper napkins from the place setting on the little table. Jeffrey had gone to some trouble to appear sincere.

Winters said, "If you're through, let's go."

"Downstairs?" Etta patted her forehead with the shredded napkin she'd been using to blow her nose.

"Yup. Go on down. I'll follow you."

I stood and gripped the table as a bit of dizziness overtook me. Taking a deep breath, I squared my shoulders and followed Etta down. Winters brought up the rear. On our way, we passed another uniformed cop with a roll of yellow crime scene tape. He grunted as he edged past us.

Once we arrived in Etta's condo, with the permission of the police officer, both she and I used the facilities. Etta got us each a glass of water from the kitchen, including one for Winters. We plopped onto the couch. He stood by the door.

Etta lifted her skirt and examined the scrapes on her legs. None of them were bleeding, though they looked close to it. She dropped her skirt and checked her arms. "I know I'll have bruises all over my arms. He squeezed my arms so hard when he was dragging me."

I nodded. I'd rinsed my mouth out when I was in the bathroom and thrown water on my neck and face. The shaking in my legs and arms had all but ceased. My eyes met Etta's. "I'm so sorry."

"You said you had a lot to tell me—"

"No talking," Winters said, his face screwed up into a frown.

I shrugged at Etta. I hoped she'd still speak to me after I told her that I'd suspected his motives. Still, everything happened so fast that day that I'd barely been able to put it all together myself.

After ten more minutes, another police officer came. This one had more decorations on his uniform. "Which one of you is Mrs. Downs?"

Etta said, "I'm Henrietta Downs." She wobbled toward him, balancing herself by touching the furniture as she walked.

"My name is Higgs. I'm sorry to inform you, ma'am, but your husband died in the fall." He glanced in my direction. "I understand you shot him? And Winters, here, says you have the weapon in your purse?"

"He was trying to throw her off the rooftop," I said. "Etta, show him your scrapes."

"You'd better not say anything until we get you downtown," the cop said to me. From his uniform, I thought he might be a lieutenant.

My stomach churned in spite of the fact that I knew the drill. It wouldn't be the first time I'd been taken downtown or even arrested. "Yes, sir. As soon as I get there, I want to make a phone call."

"Do you have anything other than your purse to take with you?"

"That's it." I glanced at Etta.

"I'm coming too," Etta said. "It's customary to get a statement from everyone who was present at the time of the incident, correct?" She looked at me. "I watch 'Law and Order.'"

"If you don't mind, Mrs. Downs, let me just have a look at your injuries."

Etta lifted up her skirt and put one leg out and then the other. She dropped her skirt and showed him the red places on her arms. "I'm going to have some bad bruising."

"Why don't we have the EMTs take a look at you, and then someone will bring you down?"

"All right, if you think it's best," she turned her face to me, "but I'm fine thanks to my friend here."

The supervisor looked from her to me. "We'll get all this straightened out." He turned to the other man. "Winters, the door."

"Let me get my own purse," Etta said, stepping over to the hall tree. "Now I'm ready." She stumbled as she walked outside. Lieutenant Higgs assisted her to her feet.

I preceded them down the hall, appreciative that I hadn't been cuffed. The scene, as we departed, felt so anticlimactic. That was okay with me. But-for a couple of minutes, things could have turned out very differently.

Chapter 23

AFTER I WAS SETTLED IN AN interrogation room, they let me call Ben. I left a voice mail. After that, I asked Lieutenant Higgs if he would call Andy Crider. Andy could probably be some support. Higgs gave me a sidelong look but agreed he'd call the deputy.

"Now, Miss Davis," Higgs said. "Mrs. Downs is here in another room. She's making a statement. I understand you have your private investigator's license?"

"Right. I'm from Houston. But y'all have my purse, so you've probably gone through it and found out all about me."

His smile was like that of a mischievous boy. "You did hand it over voluntarily." He was a stocky, muscular man with a blond receding hairline.

"Yes, I did. But I'd like to have it back. And my .38 as soon as y'all are through with it."

"That'll be a while. You want to tell me what happened?"

"You going to read me my rights?" I could only stall so long. I was hoping Andy would show up pretty soon. I knew Ben would be a while, since he had to come from Houston.

"Okay." He grew serious. He pulled a card out of his wallet and read off it, which showed he was not a sloppy person.

"Thank you. I'm waiving my rights. You have a form for me to sign?"

He shook his head in disbelief. "You've thought of everything." There was a knock on the door, and still another officer entered and handed a sheet of paper to Higgs who put it in front of me.

I signed and dated it and gave it back.

"Now, Miss Davis. You ready to make a statement?"

"You can call me Mavis." I glanced at my watch. What was keeping Andy?

"I'll just stick with Miss Davis." He crossed his powerful-looking arms and stared at me.

"It's a very long story, which I've been involved in for a very short period of time. If Deputy Crider were here, he could explain some of it."

"Crider's here, but I want to hear your explanation." He didn't even add the *ma'am*.

I glanced at the mirrored window. "Could I have something to drink?"

"We'll get you some water in a few minutes. Just start talking... please." He scooted back in his chair.

"I appreciate your being patient with me. I've had a hard day." I ran my fingers through my hair. I imagined I looked like a shipwreck. Probably smelled like one too, after sitting out on the roof for so long. "Okay, so last Thursday, I think it was, this little woman came into my office in Houston and asked me if I'd come down here and help you all solve the murder of her brother, Captain Charles Edward Linden." I figured he wouldn't like my phraseology but couldn't avoid having a little fun.

212

The lieutenant's face had already lost its hint of a smile, now replaced by a scowl. Doing my best not to laugh at his reaction, I continued. "She said her brother had been axed to death five years ago, and y'all couldn't find the killer." I took a deep breath. My mouth really was dry. Where was that water?

"So you obliged her and came down here to help us out." Definitely there was a note of sarcasm in his tone.

Counting on my fingers, I said, "Well, one, I did some research before I left Houston, whatever I could find on the internet. Two, the next day, last Friday, I went to y'all's library, which, by the way, is a wonderful library. I did more research and found additional articles. Oh, and I met the widow earlier that morning. She was just moving into her new house."

The same person who had brought the form returned with a bottle of water, handing it to the lieutenant, who handed it to me. I uncapped it and took a long swallow. I'd rather have had a beer, but what could I do?

"Between the decedent's sister, the Internet, the library, and the widow, I have a pretty good idea of what happened the night of the murder. Or at least the facts surrounding the murder. I tried to get a copy of the autopsy, but I had to order it, so I had to wait for that to come in, which it did a day or two ago. So much has happened in such a short time, everything's starting to run together." I certainly couldn't tell him that Andy had let me see the autopsy much less the whole file. If Andy was out there watching, he'd know I had his back.

"How is this getting you up on the roof with Mr. and Mrs. Downs?" He wasn't quite impatient, but I could tell he was hoping I'd get to something meaty pretty soon.

"When I left the widow's house last Friday, a yellow BMW—who would do that to such a fun car—pulled up in front of her house. A man got out and went inside. Turns out, that was Mr. Downs."

"You knew that because—"

"I didn't know that then. I found out later. I met Mrs. Downs at Mod Coffee Shop. We became friendly, and one day I was back at Mrs. Linden's going over some things about Captain Linden's murder, and Mr. Downs came in, and she introduced us. I'd seen him from the roof of the Downs's condo, so I knew for sure he was Etta Downs's husband. I figured Mr. Downs was running around on Mrs. Downs, even though the widow Linden said they were just friends.

"Then this morning, I think it was this morning, but boy has this been a long day, I was with Mrs. Downs at Mod, and Mr. Downs came in. She introduced us and…" I watched his face as I swallowed some more water. I wondered who all was watching me as I watched him.

He gave me the side-eye again. "If you came here last Friday, you've been here six days."

"Right." I nodded. "You're wondering what all I've been doing or what?"

"We're going to have to break it down more than that. By the way, how do you know Deputy Crider?"

"Hmm, uh, I came here to the police department to talk to someone about the murder case but was basically told to go jump in the bayou, so then I found out he had worked on the Linden case when he worked here, and I called him. No, that's not right." I looked at him, seeing the skepticism in his eyes. "I called my friend, Ben in HPD and asked if he knew anyone here, and he knows Deputy Crider, so he put me in touch with him. That's what it was. Turned out to be serendipitous because he had worked on the case. That's it."

"You're sure."

"Yep. I'm sure."

"And this Ben, who I believe you called a little while ago, is who?"

"Lieutenant Ben Sorenson, my uh sort of life partner who works at HPD?"

"Is that a question?"

"No. That's who he is. He should be here soon."

"So you were already down here in Galveston, wanted to speak to someone about the Linden case, and ended up speaking with Deputy Crider. Is that correct?"

I nodded. "I was trying to ascertain where the case had run into a dead end."

"It's an open file, Miss Davis. And anyway, what does it have to do with your shooting at Mr. Downs?"

"You asked me how I knew Deputy Crider. You want me to back up?"

He shifted in his chair. He didn't appear to be having as much fun as I was. "Mr. Downs. How did you end up shooting at Mr. Downs?"

"Okay, so I met Etta—Henrietta—Downs, and we became friendly, and she took me over to see her condo. I don't know why, but she confided some things in me. People just do that sometimes. I didn't know at that time that it was her husband who was friends with Mrs. Linden. But I found out when he drove up while I was there. That's what I was just explaining."

"That's when you met him."

"No. I left before I met him. I met him at Mrs. Linden's, like I said. But Tuesday night—last night—Etta had confided that she was unhappy and thinking of divorcing him."

"And—"

"Well, anyway, once I knew who he was, the person who was in the yellow BMW, I started wondering how long Mrs. Linden had known him. Could he be a suspect in the Linden murder? I'd met or at least talked to all three of the children as well as the oldest son's partner and the middle son's ex-wife. The daughter I spoke to on the phone. I also met some weird people who said Captain Linden might have been involved in some illegal goings on."

At that point, another officer came into the room. This one was a tall redhead, his hair about the same color as mine. I immediately felt an affinity toward him. He pulled up a chair and whispered something to Higgs. Then he introduced himself as Sergeant Makepeace.

"Okay, let's just stick with Downs for the moment. We can get to some of the others later."

"Yes, sir." I drank some more water. My stomach growled. After all, it had emptied itself out. Dinnertime had to be approaching. I know it was past time for my midafternoon snack.

"You first saw Mr. Downs at Mrs. Linden's house."

"Yes. As I was driving away the first day I met her, a yellow BMW drove up, and a man got out who I later learned was Jeffrey Downs."

"Then you saw him again at Mrs. Downs's."

"Yes, from the roof. Mrs. Downs—Etta—had taken me up there to show me the view. She said sometimes—"

"Whatever. But you didn't meet him that day?"

I knew that was a rhetorical question, so I merely nodded.

"How did you know he was her husband?"

"She pointed him out to me when he drove up in his car. That's when I realized I'd seen the car at Mrs. Linden's. I mean, how many cars are like that in Galveston? He probably special-ordered it."

He glanced at the sergeant. "And why didn't you meet him that day?"

"Because I left before he came in." I looked from him to the sergeant. "Okay, I didn't want him to see me with his wife, so I left rather hurriedly."

"So when did you actually meet him for the first time?"

"Tuesday. I guess that was yesterday, wasn't it? Yeah, yesterday. I went by Mrs. Linden's house, and he came in, and she introduced us." I'd already told him that, but what the heck?

"Now we're getting somewhere. You next saw him where?"

"At Mod Coffee Shop downtown this morning. He came in when we were visiting with Etta—"

"We? Was Lizzie there with you?"

216

"Who's Lizzie?" I hadn't met a Lizzie since I'd been in Galveston. "No. Lauren. She's a new friend. She used to live next door to Mrs. Linden."

"We know who Lauren is. Used to live next door? No, she still lives out there. But you don't know a Lizzie?"

He glanced at Makepeace. "Never mind. Let's don't complicate things." He shook his head and inhaled a deep breath. "So you were at Mod Coffee Shop this morning with Mrs. Downs, and Mr. Downs came, and you met him again there?"

I nodded. How did they know about Lauren? And who was Lizzie? Anyway, I went ahead and answered their question. "Etta introduced Lauren and me to her husband. He pretended like he'd not met me before, and I pretended I hadn't met him either. After all, I wasn't hired to get involved with their problems."

"But you did."

I shrugged. "It just happened. So, anyway, Lauren and I made a fast exit. Etta had been talking about going to Kerrville to visit her elderly parents and finding a place to live up there. She'd made up her mind to get a divorce. We left because we didn't want to get in the middle of any talk like that between them."

"All right." The lieutenant leaned back in his chair. "That was this morning. Then what happened?"

"Lauren drove off in her car. I left in mine. I ran an errand and then went back to the condo where I've been staying. I needed to do some laundry because my clothes were getting to where they could stand up without me. I thought I could make some phone calls while I washed them."

"I'm trying to figure out how you ended back downtown this evening."

"I'm getting to that, honestly. So there I was, minding my own business, and someone knocked on my door. When I opened it, there stood Rumpole—Mr. Downs. Ignore that Rumpole bit. That's just my nickname for him."

"What did he want?"

"I'm not sure exactly, but he told me to quit hanging out with his wife. He said she was depressed, and he was worried about her, and he was going to take her to a doctor to address it. He kept advancing into my apartment in a scary way, so I got my .38 out of my purse and told him I'd shoot him if he didn't back off. He left."

"You had a gun in your purse why?"

"It's Texas. Besides, I have a license."

"Yeah, we checked that out. Do you always carry your gun?"

I shook my head. "Nope. I went back to my office earlier in the week and got it because I kind of felt uneasy, but I locked it in my glovebox, but then Tim came over and surprised me and after he left, I decided I'd get it out and keep it with me."

The lieutenant rolled his eyes. "I'm not even going to ask who Tim is."

"The oldest Linden son's partner."

"He threatened you?"

"No, he just surprised me at my door. I didn't think anyone knew where I was staying. It creeped me out."

"Back to Downs. So he left and you, what, followed him back downtown?"

"Not exactly." I could see the *what exactly?* expression on his face, so I continued. "I finished my laundry and called Etta to see if she wanted to have lunch. She'd asked me the other day, but I couldn't. I really wanted to see for myself if she looked depressed, not that I'm an expert or anything. She declined lunch. By then it was way past lunch time, so I went to Nick's and got something to eat. I kept thinking about the Linden case and Downs being with Mrs. Linden whose husband's murder was unsolved. Then I thought about what Downs had said about Etta being depressed. Then, just for the hell of it, since I had been in Galveston almost a week and hadn't even gone to the beach, I took a drive down the seawall to the end of Cherry Hill and was on my way back when I figured I'd call Etta and see if she wanted to have dinner later. I wasn't hungry at that time because it hadn't been that long since I'd eaten but thought we could plan to eat later."

"Would you just get to the point?" Lieutenant Higgs was getting narrow-eyed.

"Well, I really wanted to know whether she'd told him she was going to divorce him. And I really, really wanted to make sure she was okay."

"And what did she say?"

"She said Jeffrey wanted to make amends, that he was having a catered dinner delivered up on the roof. She thought he'd seen the error of his ways and wanted to make things right, which made me wish I'd told her about Roxanne. Anyway, she said she had to go, he was waiting for her."

The two men exchanged glances.

"I know what you're thinking. I was thinking the same thing. By that time, I was almost at her building, so I parked and ran up there, and he was trying to throw her off the roof. *Whew.*"

"And that's when you fired at him," the lieutenant said.

"I fired twice, and he went over the side."

"So you're a pretty good shot?" He'd been doodling with a pen and now started tapping it on the table.

"I am. Ben's always had a hard time believing I didn't have any special training—when he'd take me to the firing range—but I haven't. Seems easy to me." I grinned. "Guess I have a good eye." I didn't want to tell them what I had said to Ben, that I thought it was so easy a monkey could do it.

Both men stood. They glanced at the mirrored window. Again I wondered who was behind it. Had Ben made it down yet?

"You sit tight, Miss Davis. We'll be back in a few minutes."

I nodded. "Lieutenant Higgs. If Deputy Crider is out there, I sure would like to speak with him."

He grunted and glanced at the window again. "I'll see."

"Thank you. There's something I need to share with him."

They left and closed the door behind themselves. I stood and stretched my legs. In the last few hours, I'd come up with an idea about what had happened to Captain Linden, and there was no one I wanted to talk it over with more than Andy Crider.

Chapter 24

I **CIRCLED THE ROOM A COUPLE OF** times while I waited, suppressing a big urge to go to the mirrored window and make faces. We all knew I knew there were people on the other side. That took all the fun out of it. I had known asking to see Andy was an unusual request, but they were going to have to let me go anyway, so why shouldn't I speak with him while they did what cops do before they release someone?

Finally, the door opened. Andy, in his green deputy sheriff's uniform, hesitated in the doorway. He held a folder in one hand. I knew it probably wasn't appropriate, but I hurried over to him and gave him a hug. He kind of half-encircled my waist with one arm for a moment and squeezed. "How're you doing?"

"I'll be okay. Just jittery. I've never killed someone before." Our eyes met. "Hope I never do again."

He nodded. "Sit down."

We took the chairs next to each other. He smelled like spicy aftershave. I imagine I smelled like thrown up shrimp and perspiration. He didn't let on if that was so. He opened the folder and laid out a couple of pages. "This is the NCIC and the TCIC on Jeffrey Downs. The city ran them when I told them I thought he might be a suspect in the Linden murder."

"They don't care if I see them?"

"They want you to share everything you know."

I scanned the two reports. There was no way Etta knew what they contained. He'd been married three times before Etta, years and years ago. Had several protective orders filed against him over the course of the marriages. Almost beat the second wife to death. Lauren might not be right about sociopaths not always hurting anyone. This one did. Nothing on his record for the past 30 years. I wondered why. Etta's money? "Weird, no charges in recent years."

"Yeah. He might have laid low after his parents died in a fire. He inherited their estate."

I looked into his eyes, putting aside my thoughts on how sexy they were. "You think he…maybe set the fire?"

He cocked his head. "Could have. He settled their estate pretty quickly, got a little money, and moved away. As far as I can tell, he never went back to California."

"He did. For at least one class reunion, but anyway…"

"Hmm." He licked his lips. "Now what do you have for me?"

"I need to ask you one thing first. Who is Lizzie?"

He shook his head. "No one knows."

"Why were they asking me about a Lizzie?"

His face scrunched up. "Downs said that name. He said it to the person who got to him after he hit the ground."

"I thought he was dead already."

"Not for a few moments. By the way, you didn't shoot him." His eyes darted from mine to the documents and back, as though embarrassed for me. "You missed."

That was humiliating. My face grew warm. I covered my mouth

with my hand. So much for me being a crack shot. Ben was going to have to take me back to the firing range. "I don't understand."

"They think he lost his balance in all the struggling with Mrs. Downs. She told them what happened."

I didn't exactly *want* to have killed him. I've never wanted to kill anybody. "I didn't even hit him?" I'd thrown up my lunch for nothing. I glanced at the window, imagining the other police officers laughing at my expense.

He grinned. "So now, you need to tell me what you know—or what you think you know. You have a problem with that?"

"Well...I don't have any proof, Andy, but I'll tell you what I think for what it's worth." I exhaled. My hands shook a little. I was hoping he wouldn't think my idea was stupid, though now I felt validated with the question about Lizzie. Andy remained quiet, patient, which I appreciated. "Okay. So I may have told you that the oldest Linden son, Chuck, is an alcoholic?"

"I don't think you did, but okay."

"He didn't start drinking heavily until after his father died. He hated his father. You probably know about him being adopted, and his father embarrassing him in front of a lot of his friends when the captain found out he was gay?"

"So you think Chuck killed his father?"

"No. But he's become a miserable drunk, and his partner, Tim, goes and gets him almost every night at one bar or another. Tim's kind of afraid of him now too. He told me Chuck's gotten worse since I showed up."

"You think it's Tim?"

I laughed. "No. I'm just trying to explain." Feeling cramped, I got up and rolled my shoulders back and sat down again. "And then there's the middle child, John Linden—John Wayne Linden—who was there the night of the murder but claims he didn't hear a thing. He used drugs then, though not when his father was around. After his father died, John Wayne's drug use grew way worse. I think he's into opioids probably more than anyone knows. He said he was hit by a car when he was on his bicycle recently. He's in a wheel chair. You and I both know opioid addicts are capable of injuring themselves in order to get more pain killers."

"Since he was there the night of the murder, he could have done it."

"Yes, but his wife and baby were there too, and somehow I have a hard time believing he would ax his father to death while his family was just upstairs."

"He could have been an accomplice."

"Yes, definitely, but let me finish. I talked to Vonnie, John Wayne's wife, who told me she looked out the window and saw someone running across the sand dunes. Did she tell y'all that?"

He shook his head. "I'd have to check the report, but I don't remember that. You think that means something?"

"Maybe, but I think she was lying to throw me off. So, anyway, John Wayne's drug use got worse after his father died. His wife left him and took the baby. They were divorced. He has only limited visitation with the child, which tells me the evidence of drugs must have been pretty strong sometime in the last five years for the judge to limit his visitation." I crossed my legs and leaned back, trying to relax. "Then there's the youngest child, the sister, Hannah. She hated her father, but she wasn't anywhere around as far as I can tell. She's estranged from the family, except for limited contact with John Wayne. Why is she not in contact with her mother now that her father is dead?"

"Ha!" He banged his fist on the table. "You think Roxanne Linden killed him."

"Yeah, I do."

Andy shook his head. "I don't know—"

"Let me finish. You probably know Linden abused his wife—he was pretty abusive one way or the other to everyone in the family. I think after years of tolerating his physical abuse and at least *anniversary* rapes, Roxanne couldn't stand it any longer. She had plenty of pent up anger and went a little bit mad, knowing each time he returned he would let her have it. She might have gotten the idea about the ax from her son buying one. Maybe she thought it would cause confusion." I looked into his eyes to see if I could tell what he was thinking, but of course I was distracted by them. Not that I could read minds. "She had plenty of time to plan the whole thing, since Linden was gone a lot. I kind of think she has some kind of personality disorder anyway, not that I'm a psychologist or anything. Over time, she became obsessed with the idea. She plotted and planned until the time became as right as it was going to ever be."

"And her son was there to help her." He stroked his chin, his focus on the table as he thought about what I was saying. "You don't have any proof, though."

"No, but it's only logical. Otherwise, why didn't Chuck's drinking get better not worse? Why did John Wayne's drug problem get worse? Why did Hannah change her name and move as far away as she could get from her mother? And why did Vonnie divorce John Wayne and move out of town? All of them knew she did it. Does that sound crazy?"

He pushed away from the table and leaned forward in his chair, his arms resting on his thighs. "I often thought she did it too, but I couldn't prove it. Without something—anything—we're still stuck."

"I don't know about that. Maybe John Wayne could be persuaded to talk. He may not have actually helped in the murder, but my guess is he at least put the ax in the trunk of his car and disposed of it. He might talk if he's pressured. He has prescription drugs in the medicine cabinet at the house he's staying at, but if he's truly an addict, he'll have more stashed around that house. That would give y'all leverage."

"You think she had help from anyone else?"

"Other than John Wayne? I don't know. It was so long ago. At first, I thought Jeffrey. They supposedly met up at a class reunion. I have someone from my office trying to find out when that class reunion was, and whether they could have hooked up at more than one. But Etta said Jeffrey started acting different—indifferent, really—toward her about two years ago. What if Roxanne was so miserable with Skip abusing her, she took it on herself to get rid of him and after the smoke had cleared—she knew she'd get a settlement and all—went on the hunt for someone else to hook up with?"

"And finally hooked up with Jeffrey at their last class reunion."

"They were made for each other, both a bit mad."

He nodded, studying me.

"Can I tell you how I think she went about it? I think she waited until he was asleep. They'd been drinking, and he forced her to have sex. She knew he would insist on sex since it was their anniversary. He always did. She had an ax hidden. She stripped off any nightclothes she might have still had on—which I doubt—and did the deed. Then washed off, put her nightgown on, and acted out what she later told everyone."

"Like Lizzie Borden supposedly killed her parents. Unbelievable."

"I knew you'd think I was nuts if I told you that, but when they said Jeffrey said, 'Lizzie,' I wondered. Was this some ungodly joke between them? Did Roxanne put a bug in his ear to do Etta so he could get her money? So he and Roxanne could be together?"

He sat back. We both remained quiet for a few moments. And then he said, "Why'd she end up with Downs, though?"

"They dated in high school They both went to the class reunion. Happens all the time. He may have told her his wife's a trust baby. My friend, Lauren, thinks he's a sociopath. Roxane killed her husband and reaped the benefits. Now, Jeffrey was going to kill his wife and reap the benefits from that."

"So since Roxanne's involved with, or should I say since she *was* involved with, Jeffrey, maybe when we break the news to her…"

"She's pretty tough. But you never know," I said. "She might just give it up once she knows he's dead."

"You have the address of where John Wayne's staying? We can bring him in."

"I can give it to you when I get my cell phone back. So, you're thinking put him in one room and her in another, and let each know the other is there etcetera. Right?" I wasn't as dumb as they thought.

He grinned and tousled my hair like he would a little sister's. Oh well, I had Ben anyway.

"I sure hope you're right, Mavis. This is one case I'd like to close."

"I hope I'm right too. Otherwise, my only hope is Axel Waterman, who's in prison and unlikely to tell me anything."

When they released me, they had me sign an inventory of my belongings: my purse itself, my cell phone, my wallet, complete with all its contents, my hairbrush, a lipstick, tissues, keys, and the picture of Captain Linden Roxanne had given to me the first day I met her. I'd forgotten about it. My gun, they said, they'd have to keep for a while even though I hadn't hit him.

When I exited into the lobby the police department shared with the sheriff's department, Ben was waiting for me. Was I glad to see him! He wrapped his arms around me in a bear hug. "I got here as fast as I could."

"It's okay. I'm fine." I tilted my head up, and he kissed me. I needed that.

"You're probably cleared of any wrongdoing, but they're going to run it past a grand jury anyway." He draped his arm across my shoulders and gave me a squeeze. I slipped my arm around his back. "You've had quite a week."

"Yeah. This case took me places I never thought I'd go. Did you know I fired my revolver?"

"Andy told me."

"You've talked to Andy?"

"What was that hug you gave him a while ago?" His voice had a teasing tone to it, but I imagine he felt he had to mention it.

"You were behind the mirror?"

"Professional courtesy."

"How long were you there?"

"Long enough to pretty much understand what you've been through."

"There's nothing between me and Andy."

"I knew that. He's a good friend."

"Not that I didn't find him attractive." I grinned up at him.

He squeezed my shoulders again. "All right you!" He laughed. "You ready to get back to Houston?"

"I have the condo for one more night." I turned in his arm and fingered his stubble. "Want to stay over?"

"That works for me. We could have a nice dinner on the waterfront." His smile was full of meaning when he followed up that statement with, "And dessert later."

"I just need to talk to Etta for a few minutes. And I have a picture of Isley's brother that Roxanne gave me. I'd at least like to have it sent to Isley. Then there's Lauren. I want to say goodbye to her. She was a great help."

"No problem. What do you want to do first?"

"Let me check and see if Etta has been taken home." I went to the window and inquired about Etta. They'd given her a ride home some time ago. I went back to Ben. "Can you take me downtown? I'll have to get my car before we head out to the condo anyway."

The temperature hadn't cooled down in the least just because I'd been in the hoosegow. Seemed like it should have. Seemed like everything that had happened that day took place over a long period of time, that there should've at least been a season change. We drove to the little business that had sent the earlier photo of Skip. I had them scan in the new one and email it to Isley with a message that I'd give her the original when I saw her.

Afterward, we drove to Etta's condo. She buzzed us up. I introduced her to Ben. She offered us a drink, which we declined. I explained everything to her and let her thank me one more time before we departed. Finally, we had that dinner at a restaurant with a ginormous fish up high on the facade.

Chapter 25

LATER THAT EVENING, BEN AND I learned the police had arrested John Wayne, Roxanne, and Chuck, and, in Houston, had detained Vonnie for questioning.

Eventually we found out more of the details. They picked up John Wayne for illegal drug possession when they executed a search warrant of the house he was staying in and found his stash. After he was in custody, during interrogation, he admitted that when he discovered Roxanne had killed his father, he helped cover it up. He did, in fact, get rid of the ax, hiding it in his trunk and later throwing it into what he thought was the deepest part of the ship channel. For that, he'd be charged as an accessory after the fact.

When the police went to Roxanne's house and informed her about Jeffrey Downs, she broke down. They took her in and questioned her about being involved in Jeffrey's plot to kill Etta. She denied it, but when faced with John Wayne's confession, she ended up waiving her rights and confessing to killing her husband. She was charged with 1st degree murder.

They also arrested Chuck and charged him with aiding and

abetting. Chuck was complicit only in keeping the murder secret after John Wayne confided in him. Turns out, Wendy, AKA Hannah, suspected her mother but didn't know anything for sure. She hadn't been speaking to her mother because her mother had never protected her from her father. Vonnie was questioned in Houston but given a deal in exchange for her testimony against Roxanne. Exactly how all those charges will work out, I have no idea. Hate to say it's not my problem, but it's not my problem.

When I called Lauren to tell her goodbye, she surprised me by saying, "I hope you're not angry with me."

Confused, I asked, "What did you do?"

"I thought Andy told you." She gave a little laugh. "Well, since I already let the cat out of the bag, I might as well confess. Andy came to me after we'd moved here and introduced himself. He asked me to keep an eye on Roxanne and report back to him."

Annoyance tugged at me. I had thought she was my friend. "I guess you reported every action we took to Andy and the cops who took over the case from him?"

"I'm sorry, Mavis. I really do like you. I want us to be friends."

I wasn't sure how I felt about that. She'd helped me out, all right. I suppose I should have been more suspicious of her. I mean, what stranger insinuates herself into a murder investigation? I could be naive at times. "No harm done," I said, trying to sound earnest.

"You are angry, aren't you?"

"Aww, just a little shocked at myself. I thought I was a better judge of character."

"Ouch!"

Laughing, I said, "I just mean I'm surprised at myself. Surprised I didn't question your motives for helping me. But anyway..."

"Anyway, the next time I'm in Houston, let's do lunch or dinner, okay? I'll buy."

I agreed. I really liked her too.

When I called Isley to tell her the news, she yelled into the phone, "Mavis, the man in the photograph you sent me is not my brother!"

During the moments I was speechless, I wondered how I should respond. "Are you certain, Isley? It's been many years."

"I'm positive. He is not my brother—was not my brother, since he's dead."

I shivered. "I don't know what to say." If the decedent was really not her brother, I wouldn't know where to start to help her find out what happened to her real brother. "I think we'll need to call the police."

Isley was subject to a fit of coughing for more than a few moments. When she stopped, she said in a raspy voice, "All this afternoon, I've been grieving for my dead brother all over again. That dead man, that imposter, must surely have killed him years ago and taken his place. There's no other explanation."

I agreed with her. "Tell you what, Isley, tomorrow you come to my office, and we'll figure it out together. At the very least, I think we'll somehow make arrangements for a DNA test of you and one of the sons. That would prove it conclusively. Then we can go on from there. The police will probably refer us to the feds. It's been so many years. They'll have to talk to Roxanne about when she and the imposter got together—assuming she'll cooperate."

"It won't be simple, will it?" she asked. "But I know it's not him. And that explains why he cut off all contact with me back when we were young."

"No, it won't be simple, but you deserve answers. And all this is way out of my league."

So that's what we did. After a few more days, Isley flew back to California. Disconsolate, she mostly gave up the idea of ever finding out what happened to her brother. The only saving grace, though, was the knowledge he wasn't the monster who had victimized all of the "Linden" family for the past few decades. She held on to that, though last I spoke with her, she still hoped she'd get some news before she died. Of course, she didn't leave anything in her will to the "Lindens," instead choosing the Humane Society back in California.

Etta remained in Galveston long enough to settle Jeffrey's estate, including selling that ugly car. She also sold her condo, not to me though, and moved to Kerrville. She and Ian have stayed in touch. I have a feeling Ian will move to Kerrville soon too.

Ben and I are still together. Andy Crider was tempting, but even though Ben can be chauvinistic at times, I really do adore him and enjoy training him to be more of a modern man. I'm still not going to say *I do* though.

Margaret and Candy are sharing the office duties. Both of them are serving papers. Candy says she'll wear her school uniform as long as she can get away with it. She's been searching pre-owned clothing stores in hopes of finding other clothing she can use as a "disguise." Margaret dresses pretty conservatively now, which is okay too. I promised Margaret she could help with the next big case. I want her to feel valued. We've been friends since high school. I don't want to lose her.

I've decided I'll keep doing private investigator work. Though it can be dangerous, I don't think I'm the kindergarten teacher type. I'm eagerly anticipating my next client who could possibly bring in my next murder case.

Thank you for reading!

If you enjoyed *Murder and Madness*, I would appreciate it if you would help others to enjoy this book, too.

Recommend it. Please help others find this book by recommending it to friends, readers' groups, and discussion boards.

Review it. Please tell other readers why you liked this book by leaving a review wherever you got your copy.

If you write a review, email me at **susan@susanpbaker.com** so I can thank you with a personal note.

If you would like to be on my mailing list so you can receive news of upcoming events and publications, go to https://**www.susanpbaker.com**.

About the Author

Susan P. Baker, a retired Texas judge, is the award-winning author of eight novels and two nonfiction books, all related to the law. As a judge, she dealt with a wide range of cases from murder to divorce. Prior thereto, she practiced law for nine years and, while in law school, worked as a probation officer. Her experience in the justice system is apparent in her writings. Currently, she has two novels in progress.

Susan is a member of Texas Authors, Inc., Authors Guild, Sisters in Crime, Writers League of Texas, and Galveston Novel and Short Story Writers.

She has two children and eight grandchildren. She loves dark chocolate, raspberries, and traveling the world. An anglophile, her favorite locations are England and Australia where her cousins (on her mother's side) reside. On her bucket list are a trip to New Zealand, a long trip back to Australia, living in England for several months, visiting all the presidential libraries and authors' homes in the U.S., and driving Route 66. (Don't tell anyone, but she loves to browse garage sales, Goodwill, and Salvation Army stores for bargains.)

Read more about Susan and sign up for her mailing list for newsletters and other offers at **www.susanpbaker.com**.

Like her at **www.facebook.com/legalwriter**.

Follow her on **twitter@Susanpbaker**.

Made in the USA
Lexington, KY
26 January 2019